P9-CRH-539

The Dark Library

CYRILLE MARTINEZ

translated by Joseph Patrick Stancil

Coach House Books, Toronto

Original French copyright © Cyrille Martinez and Libella, Paris, 2018
English translation © Joseph Patrick Stancil, 2020

First English-language edition. Originally published as *La bibliothèque noire* by Libella, Paris, 2018.

The Dark Library is published with the support of the Cultural Services of the Embassy of France in Canada.

Liberté • Égalité • Fraternité
RÉPUBLIQUE FRANÇAISE
AMBASSADE DE FRANCE AU CANADA

LIBRARY AND ARCHIVES CANADA CATALOGUING IN PUBLICATION

Title: The dark library / Cyrille Martine ; translated by Joseph Patrick Stancil.
Other titles: Bibliothèque noire. English
Names: Martinez, Cyrille, 1972- author. | Stancil, Joseph Patrick, translator.
Description: Translation of: La bibliothèque noire.
Identifiers: Canadiana (print) 20200328662 | Canadiana (ebook) 20200328689 | ISBN 9781552454077 (softcover) | ISBN 9781770566224 (EPUB) | ISBN 9781770566323 (PDF)
Classification: LCC PQ2713.A79 B5313 2020 | DDC C843/.92—dc23

The Dark Library is available as an ebook: ISBN 978 1 77056 622 4 (EPUB); 978 1 77056 632 3 (PDF)

Purchase of the print version of this book entitles you to a free digital copy. To claim your ebook of this title, please email sales@chbooks.com with proof of purchase. (Coach House Books reserves the right to terminate the free digital download offer at any time.)

A Reader in Danger

I had decided to treat myself to a visit to the largest and oldest library in the country. I was leaving it all to chance, having reserved no books nor made a list. To be honest, I hadn't even looked at the catalogue. I was going to the Great Library with my mind open, hands in my pockets, convincing myself that, somewhere on the premises, there was bound to be a book made for me.

This book: I didn't know its title, I didn't know what it was about, I didn't know what it could possibly look like. All I could say about it was that I had never read it. It, on the other hand, had some idea who I was. It had taken note of my reader profile. To it, my tastes and expectations were not unfamiliar.

A book was waiting for me at the Great Library and I couldn't help but believe it had been written especially for me.

Before arriving, I had undertaken a sort of inventory of my personal library, pulling volumes off the shelves one by one, caressing their smooth, woven, shiny, matte, dusty, filthy covers (with a little cleaning done along the way). I had not commenced this operation for pleasure, to look back on my readings, to appreciate the breadth of my collection, or take some sort of stock (and even less for the sake of cleaning). No, in examining my library, I was hoping to get my hands on a book I had not yet read.

It had happened to me before, pulling out a book I didn't think I owned, or that I'd simply forgotten about. I'd opened it and, from the first lines, it was a done deal: it was exactly the book I'd needed. Having experienced this many times, I have come to doubt this type of happenstance is mere coincidence. The phenomenon has occurred too often to talk about strokes of luck. Rather, I believe these books had known to stay discreet, bide their time, watch for the moment I'd be free before they'd fall into my hands. I've come to believe it isn't always the readers who choose their books: in certain circumstances, it's the books who choose their readers.

This time, after three days of searching, nothing came from my library. This meant I had nothing left to read, not the slightest text, not even a pamphlet, magazine, or article. It was awful. I had to find something, and fast: my life as a reader depended on it.

With its fourteen million printed documents, the Great Library would certainly have a solution to offer me. One chance out of fourteen million, it wasn't necessarily a forgone conclusion.

Before going to the Great Library, I couldn't help myself from gathering some information. I had, in the course of my online research, found an open-access text that traced the history of the Great Library. I wasn't sure whether this text fell under history or fiction. But it inspired confidence. I wanted to take it at its word. Maybe it was fiction, but so what? A good book of fiction, they say, contains more truth than a bad book of history.

I learned that within the realm of reading, it isn't called the Great Library but, rather, the Library. Others, in the Ministry, at the most senior level, dub it the Jewel, the Marvel, the National Treasure. The word *Trésor* must be taken literally. We are talking about a genuine treasure, the treasure of the national language, the wealth of written heritage, all of the printed matter published in the kingdom and republic which, save for the exceptional loan, are not allowed to leave the premises.

I know that today there are two ways to speak of Treasure. With respect and admiration, or with emphasis and irony.

The first comes from the institution's guarantors, its learned users, those who have good reason to believe that it is indeed a treasure. All you have to do is visit the regular exhibitions of its rare and precious documents to see that. How can you not find them wonderful, these well-looked-after editions, these books with remarkable bindings, these ephemeral publications, these handwritten letters, these children's books, these artists' editions? How can you not admire these bits of the Treasure?

The second is used by smaller libraries, those relegated to the rank of subordinates, associated institutions at best. It can also be found in self-published books, all those without publishers who, despite their incessant attempts to gain legitimacy, are denied entry into the catalogue and are bitter and disappointed at being considered works without quality.

Those who mock its prestige and attack its presumed power, those who challenge its capacity to consecrate certain books and dismiss others, should know that the Library has not always been rich and powerful. The Treasure started small. At first, it was not a treasure nor even a library. From having read it, I can say that the history of the creation of the Library is a story both ancient and strange. Almost as ancient and strange as public readership, which it practically invented.

Before the invention of public libraries, readers had to procure books by their own means. Reading was for those and only those who possessed their own private libraries. You had to be rich to have reading. You had to be rich to be a reader. Not everyone had the means to buy themselves books in illuminated vellum, and the custom was to not lend manuscripts except to close relatives (in any case, only the rich were lent to).

Once he'd acquired a taste for reading, once he'd understood all the benefits he could reap from this activity, the social and cultural distinction, but above all once he'd realized he was suffering from this incurable addiction called reading, the rich reader did everything in his power to get hold of books. His quest was to feed his collection with new material in order to have weeks and months of reading ahead of him. Tall reader, short reader, good reader, bad reader, a reader's importance was measured by the size of his *library* – or, as the modern expression goes, his *personal library*.

One day in the Middle Ages, when the sky was grey and a storm was brewing, a monk deposited the 917 manuscripts of his collection in a room accessible, under certain conditions, to other readers. The Library was born and, with it, the idea that reading could be accessible to a greater number of people. The books were no longer solely private property. It was possible to imagine reading manuscripts other than one's own, texts other than those one had chosen to acquire.

'Interesting', said the King. 'I am the King and I have decided that in my kingdom we are going to make a royal library, a fabulous treasure, a treasure made of books. It will be protected, preserved, and maintained to be shared with the public and passed on to following generations. I decide that the books will be acquired for a fee, by tapping into the kingdom's funds. Books will also be received as donations. We will get our hands on the heritages of bibliophiles and erudites, as well as those of nobles and scholars. We will bribe the writers and beneficiaries to obtain their archives, their manuscripts, their drafts, their correspondences. If necessary, we will proceed to confiscations. We will seize the property of the clergy, the libraries of immigrants, not forgetting the princes' collections. Additions to the collection of the Royal Library will be made by pillaging, to which eyes will be closed in the name of the greater good. All kinds of strategies will be implemented. We could, for example, issue a decree requiring publishers to drop off one copy of each book printed in the kingdom. This will be called the legal deposit and will be quite useful for expanding the collections without spending a dime. To purchase valuable documents, we will organize fundraising dinners. An idea is coming to me for its staging: we arrange the patrons at well-set tables, serve them meals prepared by a great chef, keep the good wine flowing, and when dessert comes we sing the praises of patronage, and no one escapes without leaving us something. All these means will be good for expanding the Treasure! This expansion will require some time and money, but that's not a problem. Time we have, as we have an eternity in front of us, and money we will find. Contrary to what they say, there is always money hidden in the kingdom, you just have to know where to look and from whom to squeeze it.'

After the King, the Treasure was handed to the State, who said: 'The state is henceforth responsible for the

Library. Therefore, we are going to nationalize the Treasure. The Royal Library is dead, long live the National Library. We are going to collect all publications, from the most common to the most rare. Our mission: to establish a heritage and preserve it. We will acquire what comes out in bookstores and buy used to fill in the gaps.'

Because the National Library absolutely needs additional space, the state pushes out the walls, re-evaluates the architecture, finds storage solutions, equips it with mobile shelving, and puts systems into place allowing individual shelves to be moved closer together on a system of railings. Despite all these tricks, the stacks remain congested, the situation becomes unbearable, on the verge of explosion, and, frankly, no one knows how things might have turned out without the intervention of the lettered President.

When he is informed of the problem, he thinks, raises an eyebrow, and says, 'As of today, the National Library is in my hands, and I've decided to build a new kind of library. I can see a very grand library, which can take into account every element of knowledge, in every discipline, and pass it on to the greatest possible number of people. The library will welcome scholars, students, researchers, workers, the unemployed. All must be able to access a modernized, computerized device, and immediately be able to find the information they need. This Grand Library is a gift I'm making to the Nation.'

All the President had to do was speak and the project is launched, the site chosen, the architecture competition opened: the candidates introduce themselves, the President examines their projects, points his index finger at the name of one architect and declares, 'That's him.' The jury yields. The architect wins the competition.

From there, the move begins: the National Library is forced to leave its historic site in the old town, which no longer allows for collections to grow and no longer meets new safety standards or the labour code, to move into a new building: four vast glass towers, both classic and minimalist, laid out on an esplanade constructed out of exotic wood and surrounding a recessed garden.

The documents make their way over, and, with heavy hearts, the staff find themselves obliged to follow. They liked it over in the historic centre, which was a little cramped, sure, the offices unanimously judged to be too small, the work spaces hardly ergonomic, but this location in the heart of the capital has many advantages: very well-connected (bus, metro, commuter rail) and located in a pleasant area (restaurants, stores, parks, gardens). The staff make known their fear of ending up in a neighbourhood that is distant, industrial, dead. They have absolutely no desire to work there, where it is so isolated. Not to mention we could lose readers, have you thought about that? What if they can't find the way to the Library? Or they give up on the new site because they find it too out of the way, too difficult to access? Imagine. No more readers? A deserted reading room? It would be catastrophic. We'll ask you one question: a library without readers, what is that? What's that called? Well, okay, it's still called a library, according to Management, peremptory as usual.

Despite the protests, the fighting, despite the increasing number of actions and general meetings, despite the threats of strikes, the leaflets, the petitions, despite the virulent exchanges and savage words, the Board does not yield, it reinforces its position: the move will most definitely take place. It must be said that the protestors were contesting a powerful argument: by moving, the National Library will change scope, it will become the Great Library. Narrow minds, what do you have to say about that?

In their place, I wouldn't have known how to respond. Neither did they, I understand, because construction began in a silence that read as approval. The President, old and sick, is knocking at death's door and, so that he can see the Great Library completed, so that he can inaugurate it, everything possible is done to make sure the building is delivered in time.

The building is hastily constructed, and design flaws will long hinder its proper functioning, but here we go, here's the President, he inaugurates the establishment, a plaque is laid, the Great Library is open.

The Great Library is established in a slightly decentralized neighbourhood of the capital, at the edge of the opaque river. As an effect of its arrival, a former freight yard is transformed into an innovative, bright, and attractive hub. What banging adjectives! Personally, I never would have associated them with public readership (though at the same time, I'm not in the business). In any case, they had been put to use on asset management and investment banks, as well as financial services; they produced results with leaders of employee savings plans, who were equally targeted. All of them felt so in tune with these adjectives that they did not hesitate to leave their headquarters and set up buildings made of glass and steel, signs of their power and their willingness to stay at the forefront of research and innovation. Right or wrong, they believed they were gaining a competitive edge. The moral: never underestimate the power and conviction of these adjectives, *innovative, bright,* and *attractive.*

Let's continue on this note. Without fear. Speak little, speak well. Speak university-business partnership. Let's say that universities had been invited to come together to form a campus, and even better, a campus of excellence, both hybrid and virtuous. A campus of excellence, which will act as a true interface between the university community and the most flourishing professional sectors. For the recreation of employees and students, they built parks with artificial turf they named after the titles of poems, books, philosophical, ethnological, sociological, and historical essays. The Ministry of Sports settled in the neighbour-hood, bringing with it some affiliated organizations. The ground floors of the buildings were rented to ready-to-wear chain stores. A large beauty-product chain set up a boutique. Fast-food franchises took advantage of attractive rents to open new outlets. Next came architecture offices, an arts centre, a bookstore, a boutique specializing in winter sports, a piano dealer, plus a multiplex with sixteen screens.

In cafés and small restaurants, rows of books popped up just for appearance's sake: small decorative yet depress-ing collections, poor publications that no one consults, no one flips through, no one touches, that prematurely wither and age beneath the indifferent eye of clients who prefer reading the menu. Is it an optical illusion? Could it be books on wallpaper? No, these are indeed physical books. Dead books.

The general consensus was that this new hub was a great success. The architects and public authorities were pleased to have created a place that was radiant, spacious, open. They didn't want to hear any more about the grey towers, the warehouses, the industrial harbour, the ill-conceived streets, the landscape of sheet metal and zinc, except comparatively, to say how significantly better every-thing was now that it had been rebuilt.

Some years earlier, poets had sung the praises of these paths that led to nowhere. Those roads where poets took pleasure in losing themselves had been transformed into clear lanes, pedestrian paths, paths busy enough for today's businesses to love. This was done so we'd forget the sheet metal, the zinc, the poets strolling about in streets lined with shelters. They said that by loitering along these paths that led to nowhere, the poets had ended up disappearing for good, which is a convenient way of eliminating them from history. As for me, I would say that this landscape of sheet metal and zinc traversed by workers and poets did not completely disappear. To find it again, one can always lose oneself in books. I know what I'm talking about, I spend my life inside them.

According to my information, the Reading Room of the Great Library sees a considerable crowd. To be sure to find a place, it's best to go right when it opens.

At 8:45 a.m., I cross the avenue to get to the light grey wooden square where there is a white block called the multiplex: sixteen rooms for just as many films. *Multiplex* is a recent word which means cinema. It doesn't mean anything different. I preferred *cinema*. One day, perhaps, the word *library* will be deemed outdated. It will be replaced by another. I prefer to not be around to hear such a thing.

On the square, people circulate in uniforms of charcoal, black, navy. Cup in hand, headphones over their ears, or their minds on their phones, they're in the process of sorting out details relative to the organization of their day, they're taking advantage of their last moments of freedom to listen to music and consume energy drinks. I think they have the look and style of middle managers or employees, but who's to say that they aren't readers? Certainly not me, who is claiming to be one. Because who knows how to recognize a reader when he's on his phone and drinking an energy drink? How do you recognize a killer without his weapon? A reader without a book? Once again, I don't know. The only thing I do know is that we're all going in the same direction. We pass by the multiplex, the wind picks up, the towers rise in the distance, I inhale, my heart is beating, I advance further still, *four glass towers with an aesthetic that is classic yet minimalist*: the Great Library.

The first tower is comprised of novels, the whole family of novels. Found there are the old classic novels, the contemporary classics, the mid- to long-term bestselling novels, all the subfamilies of legitimate novels, to which is added all the novelistic sub-genres: Novels about the Past, the Present, Novels for the Future; Fan Novels, Sports Epics, Technological Fables, Uchronia; Self-Writings, Earth-shattering Confessions; National, Regional, Urban, Suburban, Rural, Stateless Writings; Novels with Police and Vampires; Novels that Make You Feel Good, Inoffensive, Super Nice; Novels that are Disturbing, On Edge, Mad; Novels that are Weighty, Chatty, Interminable; Novels to Read on the Train, to Enjoy at Home, Comfortably Settled into an Armchair, in a Hospital Bed. More surprisingly, this tower also contains essays that aim to clearly respond to society's questions, to help with its personal growth or, in a short hundred pages, provide you with the keys to success. Lastly, the tower holds collections of classical poetry and volumes of lyrics from recent popular songs. Despite the presence of essays, poetry, and lyrics, this first tower is commonly referred to as the Tower of Novels.

The second tower gathers together the sciences, in the broader sense: hard science, physical and natural, Earth science, but also human and social science, to which is added criminology and law, the history of technologies. The tower also houses fiction that is derived from these sciences, supplementing or responding to it, which is why Science-Fiction, Biofiction, Geophysical Operas, Post-Human Speculations, Utopias, and Heterotopias can also be found here. Logically, this second tower has been baptized the Tower of Sciences and Humanities.

Unlike the previous two, the third tower is not dedicated to the storage and conservation of pieces belonging to larger and smaller categories of knowledge. It contains a wide array of genres that have in common the fact that they all belong to niches or super-niches of general literature. Whether they are without scientific backing or lack intellectual legitimacy, these are secondary books, which seem not to have been written but rather thrown together: outdated textbooks, improbable treatises, delirious catalogues, wild theories, books that are crazy, unacceptable, badly compromised, in the grip of incurable diseases. A whole series of publications whose intention is obscure, their composition astonishing, their genre problematic, and their language bizarre. This is the Tower of the Unclassifiables.

The fourth tower benefits from special protections: it is where the rare and precious documents are kept: stamps, bibles, parchments, high-quality editions, and documents of great historical value. In this fourth tower are also the personal libraries of writers that the Great Library has purchased or received as gifts. More so than the others, this last tower is subject to a close monitoring of its temperature and humidity. Without even mentioning fire, a simple bacterium can prove destructive to these precious documents. Officially, this tower bears the name Tower of Heritage. But when they speak of it, the employees and readers simply say: the Reserve.

This distribution of the collections is not simply the result of sorting the works by type; it corresponds to the turnover rate.

Those in the Tower of Novels are by far the most requested: on average, between 1,000 and 1,500 volumes are consulted each day. The readership is composed of students, teachers, the unemployed, the employed, the retired, high-schoolers. They come to inquire about one or multiple books likely to answer questions they're not sure about, to satisfy their curiosity, to quench their thirst for learning, or to bring them pleasure. These are Novel Readers, that is to say the people for whom reading is strictly limited to the novelistic genre. Of course, they are on occasion appreciative of rare editions, deluxe editions, copies annotated by renowned writers or fitted with pretty dedications, signs of an intellectual friendship between two eminent persons. But this aesthetic taste for the book object cannot distract them from the primary subject of their attention: the tale, the characters, the story that carries us away, makes us travel, amuses or torments, distracts, questions, instructs, edifies, comforts, worries, questions, or reassures. From their point of view, only a novel deserves to be given time, only a novel is worth reading. The Novel Readers are not only interested exclusively in one genre, but in a limited number of titles within that genre. The best books are the most read, and one commonly held idea is that it is precisely because they are the most read that they are the best. Wide reading prevails: here, the readers read a lot but rarely the same book twice. Except in exceptional circumstances, the death of a novelist or the anniversary of their death, the readers of the Tower of Novels never revisit a text.

According to the most recent data, between 200 and 300 volumes leave the Tower of Sciences and Humanities every day to find themselves in the hands of a public made up of researchers, students, or enlightened amateurs. The works from the Tower of Sciences are the subject of in-depth study. Their readers go through them carefully, while taking notes, not hesitating to go back if necessary, to look over the same chapter several times, the same page, the same paragraph, in order to better understand a concept's formulation, to clarify a complex idea. A title can be requested and read three or four times, or more, by the same reader. Unlike in the Tower of Novels, extensive reading is practiced in the Tower of Sciences.

The day when more than 100 volumes leave the Tower of Unclassifiables within the span of twenty-four hours will be a milestone. Like the contents of the tower itself, its readership is varied, heterogeneous, difficult to define and even more so to describe: let us list pell-mell and without concern for exhaustiveness the researchers who work in niches, the individuals keen to find a publication by an eccentric great-uncle, lovers of experimental poetry, plus a whole range of those who are curious, asocial, sick, lost, or weird. Their methods of reading are so varied that it is almost impossible to find a constant: studious readers rub shoulders with those who are browsing, some come to find a text that cannot be found elsewhere, others seem to have requested a book at random, typing into the catalogue the first word that comes to mind, selecting the first item to appear, before sitting down, placing the book on the table, opening it, and diving nose first into the opening paragraph.

If the books of the Tower of Heritage are by far the least consulted, it is due to the conditions for access. A preliminary request must be made to the Chief Curator, describing one's motivations, attaching a CV, and not forgetting to specify one's affiliated institution, publications, and research. In the event the request is accepted, the consultation will take place in a reserved room, under the surveillance of a staff member who will make sure the rules are followed: notes taken with a grey pencil (it is forbidden to use a pen, even felt-tip), the wearing of silk gloves, and limited consultation time. The readers from the first three towers should be under no illusions; The Tower of Heritage is not for them. It is only the scholars, the learned, the lettered, and the researchers who have the right to access the heritage collections. One doesn't come to the Tower of Heritage to read, but rather to gather information, make progress on work, and also, experience has proven, to commit larceny.

It is 9 a.m. I descend the metal stairs, slide in between the revolving doors, and get in line, where I see individuals in black, grey, and navy suits finishing up their drinks, concluding their telephone conversations, and unplugging their headphones. As for me, I shuffle along, step by step, until reaching a checkpoint where I yield to the security agent who demands in a monotone yet firm voice that I open my bag. While he examines its contents, I pass through the metal detector, behind which the security agent signifies, with a nod, that I am authorized to recover my belongings. I conclude that all is good, I've successfully passed the tests of the metal detector and bag control. I am admitted into the Library.

It's hot inside the hall. As I open my jacket, a light panel catches my eye. It's indicating the direction of the Reading Room: I follow it. The path is laid out with deep pile carpeting, and large windows offer up a view of the rectangular garden down below. I blink. A glass door opens and closes automatically behind me: here I am, in the Reading Room.

Silence.

Like that of places of worship, this silence is scary, intimidating; it inspires fear. What punishment will befall he who dares break it? I'd rather not think about it. Even if the Reading Room is situated in a building whose shape is reminiscent of that of a cloister, we are not in a church, we are in a room devoted to the public readership. The silence that reigns here is devised especially for reading.

There once was a time when the Room was noisy, the Library sonorous. Reading was done aloud, recited. Texts were read, played out, performed. The reader-performers vied to be the most clever at engaging an audience. The Library was frequented for both reading and listening to reading, where the text is revealed during a reading done out loud. But it was also frequented just to pass the time. It was known that one could find friends here, meet people. It was a living space, where it was nice to socialize. While the readers worked, the non-readers talked, shouted, cursed each other. If things needed to come to blows, they came to blows. The monk in charge of the Room's surveillance let it happen. In the absence of internal regulations on which to rely, he did not feel entitled to intervene; he read in his corner. At that time, the readers and the books were accustomed to the agitation and noise. When, one day, a big voice thundered.

QUIET!

Who's talking?
It's the Book.
It's expressing its anger.

I am the Book
I am the one you study
I am here to inform you
My study requires silence
You are asked to read in your heads
Here you will no longer perform
Here you now stay quiet
At the library, from now on, you will now read in silence
Keep quiet! Heed my Words

As the Book's words resonated throughout the Reading Room, silence fell. It fell abruptly. And from what I know, no one has ever lifted it. The walls would have trembled. Personally, I have a little trouble believing that the walls really trembled; it is, however, very likely that the monk had indeed been terrified by this call to order. It was his master who spoke. Because the Book was his master, the voice of his master, the instrument of communication with Him, the man upstairs, he who sits atop the hierarchy of gods and men.

For fear of punishment, the readers present in the room hunched their shoulders and plunged into the Text, of which there were fortunately multiple copies.

From that day on, the monk kept a close watch on reading behaviour. The reader had to comply with extremely strict rules of conduct:

• eyes on the page and the tongue mute;

- the left hand stabilizes the book while the right is tasked with turning the pages;
- read in silence, potentially in a hushed voice;
- the text may be muttered aloud in order to better memorize it but without turning away from study of the sacred object;
- it is forbidden to chat, forbidden to do anything, reading mandatory.

Following the Book's example, the other documents requested (and were easily granted) to also be read in silence. Even if some of them did not merit such consideration, no one would have taken the risk of going against the will of the Book. Its anger had been burned into their minds.

Silent reading was adopted, and calm and silence became part of the common good, imposed on readers in all libraries. As elements of heritage, everything in the Library should be preserved, for the benefit of all. That's why, in moving, the Library not only transferred its physical collections but also brought along its silence.

Like the books that were organized in the new stacks, this ancient silence, of great quality, had also been placed in the new premises. So that the new Reading Room benefitted, right from its opening, from a fabulous silence. The second part of the Treasure.

Henceforth, one section of the rules forbids conversations and ringtones. The new Reading Room tolerates the rustling of a page, computer and office noises; the beep of a scanner deciphering a barcode, that's fine; the rolling of a cart transporting books still passes; in a pinch, documents falling on the carpet; the pipes; the hum of the air conditioning, we have no choice; and clicks are allowed. However, as for the rest, the rule is the following, a simple rule, two words that everyone can understand:

QUIET, LIBRARY.

An ergonomic space with an adaptable and welcoming body of glass, aluminum, and gleaming laminate, the reception desk is not only the first place of contact with the reader, it also reflects the Library's values. Designed as both reception and an operative workstation, it allows agents to perform some of their daily tasks while offering a personalized welcome to the public.

A computer is sitting on the counter. A woman is seated behind the screen. Her fingers stroll across the keyboard. She is dressed entirely in red. To her side, a cart with stacks of new books. In front of her, a sign: BIBLIOGRAPHIC INFORMATION, REGISTRATION. I head toward her and say:

'Hello, I'd like to register.'

This woman in red, I feel like I know her, I'm not sure from where, but she seems familiar. I mention this to her.

'I bet you've read the text about the Great Library! I'm in it, in fact I'm one of the secondary characters. I appear as the Neutral Librarian. You know, the unassuming and docile person, the gal who does the same work every day, carries out the same tasks: she pushes a cart between the rows, she reads at the circulation desk, she gives materials to the users, she reshelves the monographs and journals, she reorganizes the bibliographic records. During her morning break, the Neutral Librarian systematically sips a tea, at noon she eats a soup, and tea again at 4 p.m., which she accompanies this time with dry cookies. At the end of the day, she takes the bus back to her one-bedroom apartment, which she shares with Incunabula, her most faithful companion, her old cat whom she adores and whose nickname is Cucu or Cuni. You think that's funny? Me, not so much. In this text, I am described as a woman who is serious and hardworking, but also a bit sad, dull, stooped over, always poorly dressed, and with the wiry body of a vegetarian hiker. Not really ugly, more just unattractive. The woman about whom they said, when she was younger, she wasn't so bad; younger, she was almost pretty. The adjective "dusty" is the one that first comes to mind to describe her. Dusty, sad, dull. In one word: librarian.'

Short laugh. Silence. Awkwardness. Breathing. I try to regain composure. Clear my throat. Silence. Breathing.

'Well, the pathetic person I just described is not at all me. Fortunately, it doesn't resemble me in the slightest. First off, I am not the Neutral Librarian – the Neutral Librarian does not exist, that is a myth or a common misconception. Call me the Red Librarian. I am not confined to an old maid's profession, thank you very much. The problem is that my profession is not well understood. It lends itself easily to caricature. Even readers don't know what my work entails, and just imagine the others, the ones who don't read. They take me to be a nun, an autistic, or a guardian of the Room.'

I appear serious and concerned. Maybe I should say something. I cross my arms. Silence. Breathing.

'Contrary to what most readers believe,' continues the Red Librarian, 'a librarian is not paid to read. Some are still convinced that my job is to read all of the books in the catalogue, which is crazy to think. In people's minds, when she isn't reading, a librarian classifies the books, gives two, three pieces of information, calls the talkers to order. A little welcoming, some information to help with a biblio-graphic search. The rest of the time she's daydreaming and yawning. There you have it, what everyone thinks about a librarian's work. Nonsense.'

I agree with a nod. Smile. Stop smiling. Silence. Breathing.

'Since it seems to interest you, I'm going to explain to you what it is I do. My work requires a great number of expertises, all complimentary to the art of reading. I want to clarify that I am an agent to the public readership, not a professional reader. Do you have any idea how many documents there are in this establishment? Do you know how long it would take for a person to read them all?'

Well-informed, I offer a number: 150,000 years.

'If you say so! 150,000 years, that seems like a lot. Anyway, life is far too short. In the absence of reading every monograph and journal issue we've chosen and shelved, we can at least describe them. For each title, I write a complete bibliographic record: title of the work, author or authors' name(s), place of publication, name of publisher, copyright year, legal deposit, name of imprint, collection name. I measure the format, note the number of pages, note the language in which the publication is written, not forgetting to specify whether it's in the original language or a translation. Does the publication have an index? A bibliography? A works cited? If that's the case, I will mention them in the record, going as far as to indicate between which page numbers the bibliography can be found. To finish, I use plain language to describe the content in a few keywords, subject headings, subject terms. One clear example: *Literature – France – 21st century.*'

I look down and stare at my feet. Silence. Holding my breath.

'Thanks to these operations, each reference can be easily found and communicated. It should be no more difficult to get hold of a famous document than an unknown one, that's the principle, no special favours or privileges necessary. You are here in a public library. Each monograph, each incoming journal receives an identical treatment. Over the course of this operation, an unwavering focus is required, without which there is a risk of making mistakes, dumb small mistakes laden with consequences: a misspelled author's name, a typo in the title, and the document becomes unfindable. When I'm not doing bibliographic descriptions, I give information to the public, I help with research, I implement actions for the enhancement of collections, I organize trainings for readers, I create bibliographies, I develop projects, I launch innovative actions, I do a thousand things about which you have no idea.'

I wasn't expecting to receive a lecture. I wonder if I wouldn't be better off getting out my notebook to take some notes. Silence. Breathing.

'Wait, the best is yet to come. What I've previously told you was a bit boring. Now you're going to get a kick out of this: when I finish my work, I evaluate it, no, but listen to this, I self-asses – that merits a laugh and yet it's no joke. I self-asses, I self-ass-es. I don't think I'll ever get tired of that. I wonder who could have invented this verb, someone who's not quite right, that's for sure. I self-asses, which means: I produce reports about my own work and potentially that of my team. The supervisors, no matter whether state, region, or city, all love self-assessment reports. It's their vice, their favourite type of literature. Regularly, they'll place an order for a text that's long, or even longer. They tell me: you're going to do a report based on your activity, we want to know everything, historical, the current situation, and please add a prospective vision. The theme? The library of yesterday, today, and tomorrow. Go crazy. Write us a tome. The Big-American-Novel kind. A thousand pages minimum, make a masterpiece, we want a fresco. You have three weeks. One month later, the supervisor contacts you again: oh whoa there, this thing is unreadable, put yourself in the reader's head for five minutes, it's a thousand times too long, my poor girl, you get lost in the verbosity, it's crazy, this mania to develop everything, and these dialogues that don't end, hellish, especially as in my opinion the length serves no practical necessity except to impress the reader, imagine you have friends over for dinner, well you aren't going to cook them fifty dishes to demonstrate your culinary prowess, you make them three, that's more than enough; so, you're going to redo your report but a shorter version this time, be comprehensive, get to the point, don't get lost in the details, summary of a summary, think density, intensity, apply yourself, here, do a poem for me.'

Hint of a smile from me. Sincere smile on my mouth. Laughter. Relief. Librarian and poet, that seems coherent to me. Breathing.

'There you have it, I believe I've more or less told you everything about my job. Now you should be able to understand that with all this work I don't have the time to read during working hours. In the Reading Room, everyone reads except for me (and my colleagues). And it's not that I don't want to,' continues the Red Librarian, without looking at me, multiplying the back-and-forths between my papers and the form on her screen, 'on the contrary, at times I would love to have an interesting book, but I don't have the time, you see, I'm working.'

While explaining her job, the Red Librarian has processed my registration. She now asks me to verify that the information about me is correct. I barely have a name, I live in a hole, my date of birth doesn't mean anything:

it's absolutely me, I confirm 'ok'. She hands me my card and a pamphlet entitled *Reader's Guide*, saying, 'Read this.'

'9:20 a.m,' she adds, glancing at her computer screen, 'don't waste any time, go find a seat, the spaces are valuable, we can't guarantee one for everyone, the readers are bizarre, the books change, things are peculiar right now, ah well you'll find out for yourself, I wish you good luck.'

I enter a room with high ceilings, bright and deep. Large bay windows bathe it in natural light. Ceiling lights with adjustable intensity controlled by outdoor sensors supplement this first lighting source, so that brightness varies very little throughout the day. The reader who raises their head after several hours of working will have the following experience: looking out the window, they will observe that night has fallen without them having realized it. Such is the ambience that the architect desired: to create a space in which time doesn't pass, it stands still. As if the Reading Room knew neither the past nor the future, existing instead in an eternal present.

The *Reader's Guide* also states that readers do not have desks but workspaces. *Desk* is a word for a piece of furniture filled with books, papers, notebooks, folders, notepads, a whole mass of documents more or less arranged, often scattered, that respond to an order understood by only one person: the desk's owner. A desk is inevitably associated with someone. It's my desk, it's there that I think and work.

Precisely identical, ergonomic, and adaptable, the workspaces respond to the needs of today's reader. Spacious enough to allow one to get comfortable, to spread out one's personal effects, to have piles of books and various documents at one's disposal, the workspaces are equipped with a lamp whose beam defines a reading plane. They are, of course, equipped with individual sockets to allow for the charging of electronics. Unlike a desk, a workspace doesn't belong to anyone, its title deed is put up for grabs each day, it belongs to the first one to claim it.

To respond to the needs of its readership, the Reading Room will henceforth be open 24/7, 365 days a year. Upon reading this notice, I start dreaming of giving up my too-small and too-expensive apartment to set up here permanently. I would leave my job, I would leave my family, I would even forget that I have a family and a job; I would give up my personal belongings to live in the Library, with only the readers and the books for company. A small community would invade the room, life would structure itself: a meal-tray delivery service would be set up, showers would be built next to the toilets, a doctor would set up practice in an old meeting room. As long as your registration is up-to-date, all services would be completely free, except meals, which would be paid for by each reader.

I come to, I hear movement behind me, stirring, I turn around: readers, dozens of readers running into the Reading Room and throwing themselves onto workspaces like athletes at a finish line. I didn't know that inside readers hid competitors. What a fun sport, the library sprint, I wasn't aware of it before.

I'd better hurry.

I explore the room at full speed, following an aisle from one end to the other.

I get to the end of the row, I move on to the next.

I'm going from left to right, which isn't deliberate, I just don't know how to do otherwise.

I'm looking for a spot that I can call my own.

I skip one row, I skip two rows, I skip a block.

I'm looking for an empty space I can take up, an island where I can live, a cave I can haunt.

Am I dreaming or is that a spot in front of me, just there?

No, I'm not dreaming, it's a spot. Near the windows, it is beautiful, it is free, it has everything to make me happy. It will soon be mine. I approach it, I'm so close, another metre and all will be grand, I will call it my spot, oh my beautiful spot, oh my workspace.

Someone I didn't see coming places his bag on top. By the time I see it, it's too late, I've been beaten. It's his spot, he won it. I didn't miss it by much, three or four tenths of a second, it could've gone either way, what do you want me to tell you, that's how it is, that's the rule of library sprinting. I was in shape but I botched my start, my reaction time was average, I have only myself to blame, I'll do better next time, I'll return and I will win.

Swallowing my disappointment, I set out to find a spot that is nice, bright, dry, and temperate. I head into the aisles. The passageways are wide enough that users and staff can pass by each other without touching or brushing against one another. The thick, midnight-blue carpet, if it doesn't cancel the sound of footsteps, reduces it to a simple gliding. By replacing the parquet with a thick carpet, walking has been transformed into a form of glide. The reader who strolls down the aisles with books in his arms will feel relieved of some of his weight. The books that he's carrying will seem less heavy. And if, by accident, he drops them, the noise will be absorbed by the hexagonal acoustic panels placed at various points along the ceiling.

At the edge of the room, I see a forest.

Moving forward, I make out pines, birches, cherry trees, black elderberries, poplars, and oaks. A bay window stops my progress: looking down I see heather and ferns. I've reached the far end of the Reading Room, I am at the border, I am before the garden-forest which, if you believe the label, makes up the heart of the building.

They planted a forest in the middle of the library. Funny idea. If I'd had a say in the matter, I would have done the opposite: a library in the heart of a forest. One would first follow a stream across the heath, entering into a pine forest where a sandy path would lead, after a half-hour of walking, to a clearing where readers lounging in the grass are reading ripe books fallen from trees.

The garden-forest belongs to various species of animals who have temporarily settled there. The label indicates that rabbits and sparrowhawks find it a welcoming environment. But never will you see readers with their feet in the grass, climbing trees, tasting the fruits they've picked. Here, the door-windows are locked, access to the garden is forbidden to humans.

Poised on a branch, a sparrowhawk opens its beak and sings. Despite all its efforts, its song remains silent, the double-paned glass preventing it from reaching me. The animals are decorative for the readers, and the presence of the readers is incongruous from the animals' point of view. The sparrowhawk doesn't care, he continues to sing. Reading his beak like lips, I decipher the lyrics:

What a crazy idea/to have built/a library/
around my forest

I head deeper into the distant regions, making my way between the shelves. I discover islets, tunnels, and caves, I cross the region of Directories, I travel among the Phone Books and Bibliographies. In the land of Specialized Encyclopedias, I see an opening between Religions and Social Sciences, and I slip into an aisle that leads me to a clear space, beneath a skylight.

There is a workspace here, with two spots facing one another. Two unoccupied spots. I set my bag down on the first. Sighing, I take off my jacket: I've found a good spot, it is as bright and quiet as I had imagined it. I pull out the chair and sit down.

A reader, under a black hat with a wide brim and in a long overcoat, towers over me. She fixes me with her light grey eyes, speaks to me in her deep voice. She gets straight to the point, not wasting any time: she wants me to give her my spot. More exactly, she's disputing that this spot is mine. Under the pretext that she sits here every day, she claims that it's as good as hers. I don't see how this spot would be hers – to my knowledge, no one here has a reserved seat, a spot belongs to the first to sit. Okay fine, she acknowledges, it's true, I can't say that it's mine, but I have my habits, I work well when I'm sitting there, I'm very comfortable. Whereas, for you, dude (apparently familiarity reigns among readers), it's the same here or there, she argues before pointing out the open spot opposite me: be nice, take this one, and let me have yours.

I agree with her on one point: I am indeed occupying a nice spot. Since it is in situated in the first rays of daylight and at garden level, I understand it is an object of desire. I've hardly been there a few seconds and I can already say that I feel good.

It's pointless to insist, I won't give in.

Without another word, the reader sits down in front of me. She takes off her long black overcoat and hangs it on the back of her chair. The overcoat slips and falls on the ground. Its owner picks it up to put it back into place, the garment falls again. She repeats this operation more cautiously, carefully so she won't have to do it again. This time it appears to be staying. I spoke too soon, it fell again. I notice the reader has a problem with her hands. This young woman with such a slender physique has short fingers, her knuckles are underdeveloped, which complicates certain operations, including that which consists of hanging an overcoat over the back of a chair. I wonder how she manages to handle a book.

Nevertheless, the fourth try is a charm. The garment remains on the backrest. The young reader then takes off her hat and empties her bag: no notebooks, no pens, no pencils, just a laptop which she places on the table and turns on, after which, with her arms crossed, she waits for the machine to start up.

During the few seconds this operation lasts, the reader scans the Reading Room. Keeping an eye on the screen out of the corner of her eye, she lets go a bit to yawn while stretching her arms. Once the computer displays OK, she puts on a pair of headphones, curves her shoulders forward slightly, and starts tapping away on the keyboard. Her short fingers demonstrate great dexterity. Suddenly they reveal themselves to be strong, muscular, powerful. These ten fingers, they are absolutely not an impediment, I hadn't understood: their shape has adapted to certain tasks at the detriment of others. The reader's ten fingers are made for the keyboard. They must have been long and thin before, but they changed shape, they adapted to their new needs.

A book is lying on my table. That's strange, I hadn't noticed it when I sat down. I ask myself if it was already there when I arrived or if someone put it there in the meantime, when I was looking somewhere else. I lay my hand on the cover. It's still lukewarm. Which means it has recently been read. Someone has just parted with it. They forgot it, or got rid of it. They let it go without thinking twice, they lost interest in it. They should have returned it to the Red Librarian or put it on the cart meant for documents to be returned, which would have allowed it to be put back in circulation. Unless they didn't have time. They felt endangered, they were scared, they stopped reading suddenly, they left hastily, leaving the book on the desk.

I look around me as if its reader were still lurking in the vicinity. Nobody. I ask the short-fingered reader if the book is hers. With her headphones over her ears, of course she doesn't hear me. I wave my hand in her direction. She doesn't see me. I make large gestures, like cries for help. I stay invisible, inaudible. As a result, I get up, go around the table and lay my hand on her shoulder. She shudders as if, by touching her, I've attacked her. She removes her headphones and, irritated, asks: dude, what do you want? I show her the book and ask: is this yours? No, clearly not, she says curtly. She puts her headphones back on, sighs, returns to her computer. I look around me once more. No one. I take a look at the book in my hand.

Document type: monograph, printed text.
Title: *The Angry Young Book*. Author: not specified.
Place of Publication: not specified. Publisher: not
specified. Publication date: unknown.
Number of pages: 51. Illustrations: no. Format: 14
× 18 cm.
Language: French. Country of publication:
France. Index: no. Bibliography: no.
Colloquia or Conferences: no. Dedication: no.
Literary Genre: fiction, novel. Physical appear-
ance: regular print.

I'm about to put *The Angry Young Book* back on the
returns cart, when I hear a small voice.

'Hey you, reader!'

'Who's talking?'

I look around me. Everyone's working. I must have
imagined it. Looking down, I realize that the book is open.

'You mean you don't know who I am?' continues the
small voice. 'It's quite obvious. It's me, your book, the book
who's been waiting for you, the book written especially for
you. It's me you came here to read. You came here to meet
me. It's a pleasure to make your acquaintance, I'm delighted.

Well, go on, now that introductions are out of the way, read me.'

'I didn't picture you like this', I say, doubting this book is the one.

'Are you disappointed?' it responds. 'I see you're hesitating to keep me. You're telling yourself you deserve better.'

'I don't know. I don't like this title too much. *The Angry Young Book*, I think it sounds bad.'

'It may not be a nice-sounding title, but it's an honest title. It describes me well. Besides, you must know that sometimes you happen to find a book's title bad and still read it … Come on! I'm afraid of what you're going to do. If you put me on the cart, I'll be reshelved pronto! And I risk being picked up by someone else. Be very careful, you're going to regret your actions. Trust me. Remember: I'm the book written for you. I was waiting for you. So, read me.'

'Funny way to speak to a reader. I've never met a book who speaks so directly. And I don't like being forced to do anything.'

'What do you think I'm doing here, sitting on this table? I was sure you'd come to the Library. I knew you'd be here this morning. And, imagine that, I even knew where your spot would be. It was written. The past, the present, the future have no secrets for me. Like all books, I have the ability to time travel and to read thoughts. Don't be afraid, stop being so shy, relax. I'll say it again: I'm made for you. Don't fight it. Read me.'

'I leave the onus of your remarks on you. I never said you were made for me.'

'Don't be shy. I'm sure we'll get along. Read me.'

'How can you say that? I've barely just met you. I need a little time.'

'No doubt you think you know the life of books. Here, for example. I bet you think that books are happy here in the Great Library? Kept under ideal conditions, controlled temperature and humidity, here they are promised eternal life. I'm not mistaken, isn't that exactly what you think? You don't see what's staring you in the face. You don't know anything about the dangers that weigh on the books, and to what point the species is threatened. The Library is a jungle. If you want to know more, I have a very simple solution: read me.'

'Listen, I don't know anything about that. You're too insistent, I don't like it.'

'Do you know this saying: "If I let out what I have inside me, what I have inside will save me, and if I keep what I have inside me, what I have inside will destroy me." This saying also goes for you. Read me.'

'Let me think about it.'

'OK, I'll admit, I exaggerated a bit. I didn't know you would be here today. The books who pretend to read the future, believe me, it's a sham. At best, some of them manage to take a clairvoyant look at the present. And that's already very good. I tried to convince myself that you would come eventually, but I didn't know when you would come or what you would look like. I have to say you aren't bad. You smell good, your fingers are clean. Finally, a reader! You have no idea how slowly the time passed. Weeks without encountering a single one, what anguish, I don't wish that on anyone, except of course the worst of my colleagues. Once or twice a day, someone would grab me and flip through my pages. Which lasted ten seconds. Then put me down. I've heard the Popular Books claim that nowadays a book has ten seconds to excite a reader. The first lines are crucial! The pitch has to be super effective, to grab them within three sentences. What anxiety! Me, I was handled, at best; read, never. Impossible to find readers. It made me sick. As soon as someone approached the New Releases display where the librarians had placed me in order to, they claimed, make me more attractive among the readership, I called out: read me, read me, I'm made for you. For good measure, I added a short pitch: *Allow me to introduce myself. I am* The Angry Young Book. *I tell the story of a library beset by disturbing phenomena. The books are abandoned; readers turn their backs on them; the Library is giving them a secondary role. There are whispers that a project is in the works to replace the physical collections with new media. I did say* replace. *Today, a threat hangs over us, the printed ones, young and old: deselecting, while awaiting worse. They'll say that the new media won't change anything, that what matters is the text. But no, I don't agree: as one knowledgable historian said, and allow me to paraphrase: the assimilation of a text is linked to its materiality. Ways of reading vary according to media. This is why it is* necessary for the different media to coexist and not compete. The danger would be in one trying to replace the other. As for me, I stand for the plurality of readings, the diversity of written cultures. I can't remember who said that cultural diversity is as important as biodiversity, and if we destroy it we will be incapable of recreating it. I agree with this sentiment. If the person to whom I was giving my speech seemed to be paying attention, I would add: *I appear to be a little theoretical like this, but I'm an agreeable read. Deep down, I'm funny. Read me.* Alas, my arguments didn't take. They disregarded me. I didn't exist. And I wasn't the only one in this situation. There were dozens of us young books fighting for readers' favour. Some of them fared rather well, but I was part of the long list of losers. And suddenly last night, for the first time since my arrival in the Great Library's collections, someone grabbed me with authority. By his contact, the way he looked at me and held me, I understood that I interested him. He didn't just flip through me, he actually read me. His gaze was intense, his fingers were thin and deft, oh how good it was. Instead of putting me back on the display, he took me with him. There, I told myself: this one is going to read you, you're getting your first reader! Upon arriving at his workspace, I became disillusioned: a pile of books was heaped on top. And there were huge ones, encyclopedias, dictionaries ... The reader placed me on the table, not on top of the stack but rather next to it, at the edge of the table. Subsequently, the other books completely monopolized him. I heard them jeering: hey, you over there,

Angry Young Book, sorry, we were here first, this is our reader, ha ha ha, good luck, we wish you the greatest success. After that, the guy didn't show me the slightest bit of attention. I think he ended up forgetting about me, because when he left he didn't even bother putting me back on the New Releases display, the polite thing to do. Lost in his thoughts, he took the pile of books he was studying and dropped each volume off at the welcome desk, explaining that he would come back to use them tomorrow, and me he abandoned on the table. He completely deserted me. I spent the night in the Reading Room. In principle, the Library was closed to the public, yet in the middle of the night I was startled: someone took me between his hands and began to read me. His fingers smelled like tobacco, his gaze was powerful, he read fast and well: I was obviously dealing with a great reader. Before day broke, he dropped me and fled, as if something frightened him. He left me on this desk, here, where you are now.'

Suddenly the Angry Young Book falls from my hands. When I pick it up, it is already warm. And then its temperature rises, from hot it becomes boiling, and I let go of it.

I place my hand on the cover like a sick forehead. I ask if it's okay.

'I'm fine I'm fine,' it responds, 'I'm more worried about you. Allow me to tell you that you do not read very well. You need to change your method. Keep your distance. You're too close, no look at you, your nose is in the text, it's ridiculous. I'm not one of those you read like that, glued, it's disgusting. You need to rethink your technique. Pull back. Take a look around, admire the scenery, breathe for five minutes, relax. Read further back, it'll be much better.'

'You're sure you're okay?'

'More or less,' says the Angry Young Book without conviction, 'but I'll be better when you start reading me. I'm tired of talking about it. Enough! Now read me.'

'No matter how hard you try to convince me you're OK, your weak little voice says exactly the opposite. I wouldn't be surprised if you have a fever.'

I shouldn't have said anything about fever or illness because now I don't feel very well either. I put my hand on my forehead. Boiling. I'm getting hotter and hotter, I'm feeling dizzy. I wonder if this book has contaminated me. I close it. Ssshhh. It needs to rest. To remain active, I unpack my things and turn on my laptop.

Beep beep, you have messages, reading suggestions adapted to your profile. Go to your reader account and click: READ.

The Girl Who is Too Nice. I was the girl next door, the class clown. In my high school, people didn't take me too seriously until the day when, in response to a letter I'd mailed him, Tom, the singer of One-Way Street, asked to meet me. By becoming the make-up artist for a world-famous boy band, I thought I was fulfilling my dream. Tom, whom I idealized, will prove to be a bad boy who never stops torturing me. I will become his sex slave, suffer abuse…before the birth of love! Read me.

An Unprecedented Adventure. Victim of burnout, I quit working to travel the world. I've had some incredible adventures! Written in a very visual style, I am pleasant, thrilling, entertaining, full of unexpected turns. If you love adventure, you won't be disappointed. Once you start, you can't put me down! Reading me, you will experience a pleasure identical to what your favourite movies and TV series give you. If you wish to have a great time without getting riled up, you know what you have to do. Read me.

A Great Need for Love. It's been a long time since I've had a relationship. In the past, I had experiences that didn't end very well. Today I am ready again to find a new someone special. I will tell you the truths of my life. Age, distance, and background do not make a difference in my eyes. I am sociable, sweet, sensitive, and generous. I don't know what could happen between us, but I would like us to be friends. Read me.

Depressed Poem. Renowned critics have praised my originality and recognized my inventiveness. But, to be honest, I've had few readers. It's unfair, because I am the fruit of ten years of work. You may have heard rumours that I was difficult. This is not true, I am quite accessible. Well okay, I may be a little unusual, but in a normalized world, that's a quality, right? Read me.

A Burning Affair. This is the story of a shy young girl in love with books. She enrolls in creative writing courses. Her talent is very quickly spotted by her literature professor, who is also a renowned writer. After one class, he holds her back and offers to give her very, very private lessons ... With me, you will see long-term improvements in your erectile dysfunction. In the hottest passages, your penis will grow up to 15 percent! To be frank, I'm boiling hot. Come and find me quick. Read me.

Bibliometrics. John belongs at the top level of international research. At least that's what he believes. When new methods of measuring scientific performance are adopted, he is astonished to discover that he has been given a grade of B+. Little read, little cited, his texts have in reality a very low impact. To improve his rank, John decides to take up crime and disseminate the report of his actions. He will become one of the most-read authors in the world and will end up with a grade of A+, just before getting arrested, sentenced, and thrown in prison. Read me.

Just Got Out. Like many readers, you may have appreciated the earlier volumes of Romeo's adventures in search of his father. It is my pleasure to share with you the birth of volume five of my saga. For investigative purposes, Romeo goes off to visit strange lands where we will encounter creatures with strange powers before the final revelation. I am a novel of exceptional power. I'm the book everyone's talking about. I'm the one you've got to read. Don't be left out. You don't have a choice. Read me.

The Monster Library. Hippolyte, seven years old, wishes to help his father write a novel. He tells him the story of a library monster who, at night, eats books. At first, the monster eats the children's books, considered to be better because of their sweet and colourful drawings, then the adults', salty, caloric, nourishing. The monster's appetite has no limits. The more it eats, the hungrier it gets. The monster gets bigger, he becomes enormous and scary. After pillaging the municipal library, the monster then opens his own establishment: the Monster Library, paid access, books read aloud, pay-per-use, possibility for yearly subscription, hundreds of thousands of titles available on demand. I'm a book for the young and the old. Read me.

The Stranger Was Famous. Do you always respond to the messages you receive? At first it was a simple bet, she had to write to a stranger, but Jeanne will later understand that her correspondent is no ordinary person. Do you want to know who Jeanne's mysterious interlocutor is and how this simple message is going to transform her life? Read me.

The Island Was Almost Deserted. I am a story in direct touch with the facts and the meaning of life. After working for a large company, the narrator retires from business and returns to the island where he was born. We will meet a whole host of characters both endearing and compassionate. I hope that, contrary to existing criticism, you will recognize my talent. Read me.

Is There a Poem in this Class? Like every Tuesday morning, a university professor gets ready to give his seminar on contemporary poetry. At the last minute, the administration asks to change his classroom. In the one that is newly assigned to him, some names are written on the chalkboard, undoubtedly discussed during the previous class. The professor, naturally facetious, decides to keep them. When his students enter the classroom, he points at the board and tells them: this is a poem, interpret it. The students get to work. They produce text analyses that confirm it is indeed a poem. Does this mean it is the readers who make poems? To know about this strange method, read me.

The Angry Young Book. I am trying to translate this currently very common feeling of insecurity by producing a story in which readers are stricken by a new evil that turns them away from books. I am looking for readers who can understand us and support our fight. Do you want to know what's going on in this library? Do you want to help us? In this case, you don't have a choice: turn the page, read me immediately.

The Angry Young Book

Do not trust the calm and intimate atmosphere. Fear reigns over the library. Not so much among the staff, who might have feared a degradation in their working conditions, but in the books, who fear the future. Many of them express their feelings of insecurity through terrifying stories in which the readers are afflicted by a strange evil, which turns them away from books. The question of whether they'll have readers is a recurring fear among the young books. But what was until now an unsubstantiated anxiety, today becomes anguish – completely justified anguish. The young books fear being moved far from their potential readers, to the third basement level, or even the warehouses. They are afraid that after discreetly being taken far away, they will be done away with, assassinated.

The moment has come to fight for the cause of books. And the Oldies and Classics cannot really be counted on: they have done their time, they have received gratification and honours, and the majority know that no matter what happens, they will continue to be studied. They don't understand our anxieties and fears. But you, a reader, you must be capable of understanding the situation. Support our cause. Join the fight now. Read me.

When the Great Library opened, there was still something to be optimistic about. The books were happy to be in a new and functional locale. The atmosphere was good, the light relaxing, the furniture comfy. The readers appreciated being in a more comfortable reading room, more spacious and better equipped than the old one. Books and readers were living in perfect harmony. The books found an interested audience rather easily, and audiences effortlessly found books responding to their needs. The librarians were convinced that books and readers were unable to live without one another, their destinies intertwined. In the mind of a reader, 'reading' invariably meant *reading a book*. As a result, they considered themselves indispensable to readers. Survival of both species seemed assured. I am a book, you are a reader: let us love, let us unite, let us reproduce, let us live in joy and peace. Yet, after a few idyllic months, the situation deteriorated.

At the end of last year, the Library lost one of its readers. And not just any reader. By his age and his diligence, he was the one who knew the books best. The one who had read the greatest number of them. The one who had paid them the most attention. Always concentrating, he read with a grey pencil in hand, to take notes, or a pencil in his mouth, to compensate for the ban on smoking inside the establishment.

The man was a retired historian who detested being called that. 'Retirement,' he grumbled, 'makes me no longer accountable, I'm the master of my own schedule, I do what

I want, and what I want is to be a full-time historian, not a retired historian.'

The Historian possessed the qualities attributed to great readers: faithful, assiduous, monomaniacal. He said, 'A great reader, I don't know what that is. I am neither a great or a good reader, I am neither great nor good, I am a crazy reader.'

The Historian felt that he had always known how to read, which was of course false, he had been taught, but he had forgotten what the world looked like before that. He was born when he started to read, then he grew up reading.

The Historian sometimes saw a scene with a child, a book, a reader. It's evening, and the baby doesn't know the alphabet, he ends up knowing by heart the book that is read aloud to him each evening, they close the book, kiss the baby who, head full of pictures and sentences, drifts off to sleep.

The Historian compares the discovery of a book to a trip to a new city where an unknown language is spoken: you decipher the illuminated signs, you decode the animated advertisements, by reading menus you taste an exotic cuisine, with directional signs you invent landscapes, and with a horoscope you create a future. You don't read to navigate correctly, to foresee the future, or to align your diet with the local cuisine; you read for the pleasure of reading in an unknown language.

So the Historian loved books, and they loved him back. It wasn't that they were all his friends – certain books were in deep disagreement with his way of reading – however even his enemies had much respect for his life and his work. Personally, I barely knew him, but I know that for the Oldies it was a privilege to spend a moment in his wrinkled hands, to be caressed by his long and thin fingers, swept over by his charged breath. The books emerged impregnated with a smell of tobacco that marked them forever. They couldn't complain: to smell like stale tobacco is the price to pay to be read by him.

When they said *he's read everything,* they weren't just saying that, they weren't far from the truth. It was enough to spend a little time with him to know that he knew practically all of the books. I mean, he knew them personally. You gave him a title, he gave the author's name; you gave him an author's name, he recited their complete bibliography. You would have sworn that not a single book in the Library was a stranger to him. In his mind, it was clear that all the books were waiting for him to read them. This was a tremendous reader. His disappearance was a shock. It was fraught with consequences.

A few years earlier, the Historian had demonstrated his commitment to the Great Library by gifting his own collection: an exceptional array of documents, 35,000 volumes rich (monographs, journals, offprints, duplicates), not counting archives (manuscripts, letters, notes, drafts, leaflets). He had given everything he owned, the entirety of his treasure, keeping for himself only the ten books he considered essential.

35,000 volumes, the fruit of fifty years of research, arranged in an apartment 120 m^2, how was this possible? At first, the librarians in charge of the appraisal didn't want to believe it. People estimate high with their property, she said, they think they have this incredible collection, when in fact it's worth nothing, we know how it goes, we've been through it a hundred times, it's classic.

Arriving on the premises, they discovered an apartment where each wall, each partition, was covered in wooden or plastic furniture consisting of shelves holding books three rows deep.

After their assessment of it all, the librarians had to face the facts: the promised 35,000 volumes were most certainly all there. They noted that the apartment was suffering from a significant load: the wooden floor was sunken in some places, and the furniture, resting on an unstable floor, seemed on the verge of toppling over. Collecting promised to be tricky, even dangerous: you grab ten books, a shelf tips over, bringing with it one or two others in its fall, and now there are hundreds of printed materials falling on top of you. You can wind up maimed by less than that. It was a miracle this apartment hadn't already collapsed onto the one below. The couple of teachers who lived one floor down thought they led a comfortable, tidy life; however, they had risked a great deal simply by sitting at their desks to correct homework or prepare for their courses. At any moment, the ceiling was likely to give way, with tons of books about to crack open their heads and shatter their bones.

As proof that the Historian's library was not for decorative purposes, each printed text was underlined and annotated: even if he had read only one or two pages, sometimes only the introduction, one chapter, or an article whose intentions were in line with his concerns or posed a new problem for him, it was clear that he was acquainted with every document. And this was not a family library, a collection he had inherited and added to over time. Coming from a social background where one did not read, he had started from scratch, had built a collection of documents that, inevitably, resembled him, and in a certain way constituted a masterpiece in its own right.

Every document bore his mark, and the whole of it conveyed his intellectual ambition: to understand the workings of history and mankind's progress through fluctuations, changes, turning points, progress, and crises. His readings helped him grasp historical rhythms, according to continuities and discontinuities, evolutions and breaks. Apart from the Historian's interest in both planetary space and historical time, his library manifested his refusal of a primarily Western history. He thought at a worldwide scale. He wanted to know and understand the history of every country, of every region, of every era. From the beginning to today.

On top of representing a cultural memory, his library revealed this long phase of exploratory accumulation, preliminary to any research undertakings, and manifested a willingness to explore all fields of knowledge before in turn producing anything himself. Once he had read everything, he would model history, he would make an exact science out of it.

From antiquity to modernity, nothing seemed to have escaped him. He knew ancient and medieval history like the back of his hand, as well as modern and contemporary history. The historiography and philosophy of history held no secrets for him. He had mastered the history of science and technology, the history of art, social and cultural history, and, to a lesser extent, the history of religion and the history of medicine. Even in a field of minor intellectual specialization such as the history of sports, he had closely studied between four and five hundred monographs, offprints, catalogues, and thematic journal issues.

He had published a little, in the end, in light of the impressive mass of his reading. His bibliography included seventeen titles:

The New History
The System of History
The Universals of History
Where is History Going?
On the Other Side of History
A Universal History
A History Without Preferences
History and Historians
History, the Progress
The Alternations of Progress
Progress and Regressions
Turns and Periods
Are There Historic World Turning Points?
The Cause of the South
Our End of the Century
The Success of Failure
Victories Over Time

Q: One may wonder if this global history you've been looking for throughout your life does not find its realization in the impressive pool of documents you have formed through fifty years of research.

A: I have long searched for how history works, its driving force. I have searched for universal and global history, and I have come to the conclusion that, if history exists, it is in the stacks and the holdings of the Great Library that one may find it.

Of the 35,000 volumes in his private library, he had insisted on keeping ten books, the ten essential titles. To make his selection, he projected himself into the following situation:

Imagine you have to leave your home urgently, you have ten minutes, right now they are heading toward you with the intent to eliminate you, they are violent, armed, determined, don't waste any time, each second counts, it is your life on the line, you can only take with you one suitcase in which you will put ten books not a single one more, hurry up, you only have nine minutes and fifty seconds, you have to decide now, answer, which books would you take?

Over the course of his reading, the Historian had learned things that should have remained secret. He would have been better off reading a little less, keeping a little distance from the texts, from time to time skipping a page here or there, forgetting a chapter, disregarding certain dialogue, eliminating some characters. It would have done him a favour. The danger hanging over him would have been less.

With his way of reading everything everywhere and all the time, the Historian had access to names. But these names didn't refer to harmless characters in fiction, they referred to very real bad guys who were preparing to commit crimes. Listening only to his conscience, the Historian wrote an article to denounce this small seditious group and the regime of terror it wished to establish. In exposing this threat, he was hoping to dismantle the organization but also, at the same time, thwart the support it received from the rich and powerful. It was an entire criminal network he wanted to denounce. He believed in the ability of a published text to, if not kill the enemy, at least change the course of events. Writing was for him a form of action. In writing, in publishing, he knew what he was aiming for and what he was exposing himself to. The reactions could be violent. It was necessary to consider the possibility that a text could turn against its author. If writing was a weapon, it was double-edged.

He finished his article, sent it to a journal to which he had already contributed, a friendly journal as it were, whose positions were generally close to his own. Anxious to not derail his case, he had given the text in person to an old childhood friend, the son of lowly employees there who had also became a historian, and who was a prominent member of the reading committee.

The Historian thought he had taken every precaution. Yet he was wrong. We don't know how members of the group knew about the text. It seemed like the conspirators had read over his shoulder. More likely, they had an ally, a source within the journal's editorial board. And it's through this mole that they would have been informed. In any case, they learned what the Historian knew about them, how he intended to thwart the dirty tricks they were preparing and unveil the inglorious cause that animated them.

The journal was rapidly changing then. The steady decline in sales over the previous five years had created a deficit that the financier, at the head of an industrial empire left to him by his father, was now refusing to absorb. He accepted losing money. Money, for him, was not really a problem; he could throw stacks of bills out the window and he would still always have enough in his various bank accounts. But he had more trouble with publishing a journal that didn't sell, a journal whose only readers were the members of the editorial board, a few relatives, and the recipients of press copies. He argued, no doubt reasonably, that this trend could not be reversed, at least for the near future. Readers, once they abandon you, rarely come back. You've won them over one by one, you've taken years to interest them, and all it takes is one or two failed texts for them to leave you in droves.

Compelled to rethink their model, the members of the journal's board opted for a change of format (in truth they were forced to – it was that or cease publication). It is within the context of this transition from paper to digital that the Historian's text got lost, one file among many others in a database – which was, of course, as badly organized as the proverbially messy editor's desk.

Not only was the text not published in the journal, but as a result he was also placed at the top of their list of people to take out. The Historian, however, was not aware that he was being targeted. He most likely would have been executed if a friend, at the same time, had not been keeping watch over him.

One Monday, at 6 p.m., the Historian received a phone call. His interlocutor didn't give her name, she simply announced herself as *a friend*. This person's voice was not unknown to him, though he was unable to give it a face. His interlocutor warned him, without elaborating, of the danger threatening him and getting closer. He should leave his apartment as quickly as possible or risk being killed.

'Meet me in ten minutes,' she ordered, 'at the intersection of X Street and Y Avenue. I'll be in a rental car, I'll drive you to a safe place. Now.'

Although he considered it inappropriate, the Historian didn't take offence at her directness. He hesitated a few seconds on how to proceed. His article being lost, it was in fact possible it had fallen into the wrong hands. If this were the case, a serious danger threatened him. So he grabbed a suitcase, stuffed it with clothes and toiletries, and as there was still a little room, he put in ten well-known books.

Two minutes later, he was in the passenger seat of a rental car driven by the woman who claimed to be his friend. He knew that attitude and that face. The woman said something to him. However, despite all his efforts, he couldn't place her.

In the Reading Room, it would have been necessary for the Historian to look up more often to memorize the face of the one who, that day, had taken a half a vacation day to save his life. Yet you couldn't miss her, she was there every day at the welcome desk. For years the Historian had looked at her without seeing her, as if he reserved all his attention for the texts.

She pointed out that she was invisible to him, without being reproachful – when it comes down to it, that's what her profession wants: she is a librarian, that is to say, invisible. The Historian pointed out to her that he was nearsighted. He saw poorly from a distance. It was her, the Red Librarian.

The Historian put on his glasses and thought: *This route doesn't make sense. First we made concentric circles around our starting point. Then we went in a long straight line and suddenly turned right, squealing the tires. Exiting the turn, we slowed down and then for no apparent reason quickly accelerated, we turned left, left again, we entered a roundabout at full speed, sharp turn, second exit, then another straight line, then drove into a tunnel with the headlights switched off, going the wrong way. All this to return to where we started. I wonder if I did the right thing getting into this car.*

The Historian, beset by nausea, opened the window to let fresh air into the car. Against all expectations, the Librarian slowed down. She who, two minutes earlier, seemed to be engaged in a high-speed car chase with a phantom vehicle, was now driving extremely slowly, well below the speed limit. Bicycles were passing her, flashing their lights, scooters honking, all accompanying their protests with obscene hand gestures. These interventions had no effect on her manner of driving. The Librarian could give a royal shit. She continued on her way as if nothing had happened, whistling at the wheel, taking a roundabout three times around, accelerating on the turns, slowing down on the straightaways.

Exhausted by a sleepless night, the Historian yawned, closed his eyes, and finally fell asleep. He woke up when the vehicle stopped. It was parked in front of the Great Library. One could not imagine a longer route to get from Point A to Point B. Thanks to this alternative route, the

Librarian and the Historian could be certain they hadn't been followed.

'This is your refuge,' declared the Red Librarian, giving him a visitor's badge.

At 8:18 p.m., the Historian triggered the fire doors to open by applying a badge to the electronic lock. With a telephone in his pocket, he entered this space that appeared to not have clocks or windows, where the printed documents lived in peace, and was called the stacks. Before leaving, the Red Librarian warned him:

'Be very careful. Nights in the Library are not without danger: listen to my advice, do not read, do not open any books between midnight and 9 a.m., you have been warned.'

The Historian took some stairs, got into an elevator. He slid onto a moving walkway. He climbed up the ladder. He crossed partitions. Doors opened before him. He defied the safety instructions by taking a freight elevator. Although the stacks were vast, the temperature and humidity remained stable, under control, which was not lost on the Historian who, by dint of living in the company of books, shared with them a hypersensitivity to thermal and hygro-metric variations.

In the aisles, he let his gaze run along the shelves where the hardcover and paperback volumes were organ-ized by discipline, by format, and by order of arrival. He swept past the written heritage, millions of works and hundreds of thousands of authors, first editions, special editions, reprints, letters, manuscripts, letters, cards, maps, autographs, millions and millions of studied texts, commented on and annotated by hand by a researcher, dedicated by the author, texts that have become famous, others that have been forgotten, works purchased or received as a gift, or even the product of a confiscation. The Historian sank further into knowledge, he travelled among the populations, societies, social groups, territories, he passed through the sciences and technologies, languages, scriptures, arts, religions, he visited the ancient and contemporary worlds, he entered into folklores, tales, and legends.

The next day, the Historian didn't show up at the Library. Nor did he in the following days. I was very worried. It wasn't like him to be absent several days in a row. Usually, he came every day. Even when sick, he tore himself out of bed; defying medical advice, he showed up in the Reading Room with a hot forehead, wet cough, clammy hands, intrepid despite the fever. It was the historiography books he had been studying who alerted the librarians, who referred them to the head of security. He found the contact information for a close family member (in this case his daughter), whom he called.

She picked up on the first ring but took a moment to understand the reason for the call. Why was a representative of the Great Library insistently asking for news of her father? At the start of the conversation, she spoke in a flat voice with a mechanical tone, like an answering machine maybe. She wasn't really listening to her interlocutor. Her head was somewhere else. The phone call surprised her while she was in the process of working on a book.

Having studied classical literature, the Historian's daughter was now falling into the experimental. She specialized in genre affirmation procedures applied to literary works.

Through a series of complex manipulations, she transformed a poem into a novel, or a novel into a poem.

'Nowadays, it's not only humans who are transgenre,' she explained over the telephone, 'this phenomenon also affects books. We must face the facts: poems have not all chosen to be poems, and not all novels are happy to be designated as such. Often it is the publishers, bookstores, and libraries who have assigned them a genre. When we dig deeper into that question, we see very quickly that there exist poems who on the inside feel as though they are novels, and novels who would rather be poems. You see, I knew a super-virile Thriller who blossomed as Lyric Poetry. The fighting, the aggressiveness, the dirty tricks, they weren't his thing. My practice is not illegal, but it's frowned upon. You cannot imagine how upset people are with me, heaps of people hate me, I receive threatening letters every day. The literary institutions refuse to recognize transgenre texts: to them, a novel must remain a novel, a poem a poem, otherwise, they shriek, that's the end of Literature. Always such harsh words! It's painful. Too bad for them, one day or another they'll see things my way, but so much wasted time! In the meantime, I'm still not receiving any grants. So I have no choice, I adapt my rates according to the income of my clients. The Big Novels pay more than the Poetry Chapbooks, a matter of resources. Anyway, I don't know why I'm telling you all of this. Let me get this right, you're the head of security at the Great Library and you're asking me if I've seen my father recently?

Well, no, actually it's been a while since I've heard from him, but I'll do what's necessary. I'll keep you up to date.'

After hanging up, the Historian's daughter then called her father. Voicemail. Then she went to knock on his door. No response. She picked up her phone, called again and again. Voicemail, voicemail, voicemail. Out of options, she alerted the police who, after several stern warnings in a theatrical tone, broke down the door to get inside the apartment.

Empty shelves suggested that a man who loved books had indeed lived here, but given the dust, all the layers of it that made up a sort of black and viscous carpet over the furniture, it wasn't yesterday.

The police didn't notice any signs of aggression, no fingerprints, no clues. A call for witnesses was made:

AN EXPERIENCED READER HAS DIS-
APPEARED BETWEEN SATURDAY EVENING
AND MONDAY MORNING. HE IS NOT
ARMED, HE IS NOT DANGEROUS, DO NOT
BE AFRAID, HE'S A HISTORIAN. IF YOU SEE
THIS MAN, DO NOT ENGAGE, CONTACT
THE CLOSEST LIBRARY.

Weeks passed and still not a clue, not a trace or finger-print, not a witness, nor the slightest piece of information that could have put the police on track. No proof of life, no proof of death; the Historian seemed to have vanished.

Three months later, traces of him started turning up in books. The Historian had disappeared from reality only to reappear in essays and novels as a main character, a subject of study, or an object of investigation. An abundance of literature was dedicated to his disappearance. I remember that during this time any other subject seemed irrelevant, or at least secondary. In the reading community, one soon spoke about the Affair, with a capital A. I followed it carefully.

I know that the first works devoted to the Affair were journalistic accounts, investigations that, each in their own way and with varying seriousness, were looking for the key to this mysterious disappearance. We are far from knowing the truth, they claimed. This affair consisted of grey areas that, whatever the cost, had to be cleared up. The credibility of the books and their ability to engage readers was at stake. These were troubling times when, despite no one having any evidence to explain what really happened, a number of media outlets insisted on offering their opinion. Competition was fierce among the publications. This was a welcome or destructive phenomenon, which either allowed for multiple points of view or, on the contrary, normalized them, depending on the school of thought. Like in every experts' quarrel, each produced their own analysis in order to provide the community with an original perspective on a phenomenon that was at first glance unexplainable. How does one disappear from one day to the next without leaving a trace? We'd really like to know. Some of the experts produced relevant analyses, but these were drowned out by the mass of reductive assessments, incomplete information, partial judgements, even ridiculous opinions that made up the bulk of the output. But were they all even trying to be relevant? I have a feeling that the important thing was to speak loudly, make noise, produce a series of speeches, take part in the debate, even with banalities or misinterpretations.

The second wave was made up of scientific publications, conference proceedings dedicated to his work, or a mixture, in his honour. It was about paying tribute to the researcher, to celebrate the intellectual, the insatiable researcher, the tireless reader, he who, from the start of adolescence to extreme old age, stayed alive by this thirst for knowledge. The Historian was described as a scholar: one who gathers information, checks his sources, gives lectures, maintains a healthy dialogue with his friends and colleagues. He was the office historian who delivered his conclusions in monographs, in thematic journals, in colloquia. All of that gave the paradoxical impression that, despite having disappeared from circulation, the Historian remained active and productive. Without putting forward any evidence, these books implied that the Historian had gone into hiding. Voluntarily shut away, he had withdrawn from the world to dedicate himself entirely to his research. On his desert island, in his shelter, in his refuge, in his historian's residence in the country, he gathered information, he thought, he wrote.

The third wave of books dedicated to the Affair were part of another category entirely: this time they were the detective novels, the thrillers, the adventure novels. For these captivating plots, the Historian left behind the clothes of an office scholar to don those of a political activist. The detective novels, the thrillers, depicted the Historian as an active member of a small anti-colonialist group. Instead of fighting solely in the world of ideas, this time he was at the heart of operations: he carried suitcases containing confidential documents; he assembled secret meetings, plotted, instigated; he sabotaged, hijacked, infiltrated; he disguised himself; he spied, used several passports; one day he was blond, skinny, and bald, the next day he was brown-haired, thick-set, moustached (whatever his disguise, he risked his life at every turn). Having trained as an explosives worker, he occasionally blew up bridges and bombed cars. The greying academic was just a cover, under which hid a hands-on kind of man, a man who braved danger and worked out in the open, a man who was not afraid to engage physically to defend a necessary and just cause. Alas, the adventure took an unfortunate turn: undoubtedly betrayed by a false friend, the Historian was captured and then locked away in a suburban cellar. His enemies subjected him to torture sessions where they beat him: *we want information, we want information, give us names, tell us what you know. What information?* he yelled, after they had torn off his fingernails, *I don't have any information, you have the wrong person, I'm a historian.* Some of the detective novels ended like that; others gave an account of the Historian managing to escape. But his escape was short-lived: quickly recaptured, he was knocked over the head with the seven volumes of *The Tides of History*, all 4,800 pages. The Historian lost consciousness; his lifeless body was transported in the night to a deserted quay, weighted with the heavy volumes that had knocked him out, and thrown into the river's opaque waters where, weighed down by the wet paper, he sank. At any rate, this is just a hypothesis because the body of the Historian was never found. The absence of a body allowed for endless speculation, which was a way of feeding future works with all sorts of crazy revelations. Thus, one could hope to publish many other books that claimed to provide the key to the enigma, without fear of being contradicted by the facts, scientific truth, material evidence, the autopsy that would blow it all up. The only risk was that the readers would, eventually, get bored.

The Affair, in any case, seemed contained to the world of books. Hegemonic in the world of reading, anecdotal elsewhere. Off the pages, the Affair was just a micro-event to which the police paid distracted attention, focused on from afar, dispatching a small team as a matter of policy which conducted its investigation without straining and delivered disappointing conclusions. To them, a man had disappeared without leaving an address, so what? In cases like this, the guy just wants to be left alone, it happens all the time. No doubt he retired to the country where he'd rented a house under a false name, to make sure he wouldn't be bothered. You could imagine that, since his retirement, the man read the speculations about him and laughed. According to the police, they saw it every day, men who peaced the hell out. Especially when retirement came. It was tempting. A thousand narratives were built on this starting point: a guy who mysteriously evaporates and seeks to instill doubt, titillating the curiosity of thousands of readers who will later learn that this disappearance was skilfully staged, not out of malice, but from a taste for gripping police stories. But, even if the fans of thrillers could still get caught up in it, the police were considerably less enthusiastic: *not much to report*, they tell you, *no need to worry, move on, close your book, or at least turn the page.*

The problem is that the Library's readers were so caught up in the Affair that they had neglected the rest of the collections. That which didn't concern the Affair seemed uninteresting. Consequently, the number of consultations and loans fell. This felt harsh and violent. Especially for the Popular Books, who boasted about being constantly on loan, who said they were proud to contribute to the library's quite decent turnover rate, and who even went so far as to take the title *heart of the collection* for having a large and captive readership.

Even if this drop in the number of loans was bad news, I have no desire to cry over the fate of the Popular Books. To be frank, I have no affinity with them; we have nothing to say to each other, and their false modesty annoys me. And I'm not just saying that, I speak from experience – I've had the opportunity to rub shoulders with a few since my arrival at the Library. I remember one novel in particular who, built for success, spent his time methodically counting his readers and who, at the end of the week, offered the numbers with a hypocritical detachment:

'Oh man,' he yawned, 'what a week! I didn't have five minutes to breathe. I thought they'd never put me down. More than a thousand readers in seven days, that's crazy!

Look, I'm not complaining about having so many readers, and loyal ones at that. There are so many books who dream of being in my place. It's gratifying to be read a lot, but we should also recognize that it's exhausting in the long run. Oh, if you only knew, it's not always so easy being popular, but what do you want me to do, I can't prevent people from liking me. Anyway, luckily I have Sunday to rest up. And you, how's it going? Did you have a good week?'

And suddenly, overnight, readers no longer paid the slightest bit of attention to the Popular Books such as this one. They didn't look at them, they no longer touched them. A terrible experience for these books, who had ended up believing what they'd always been told: *if you are popular it's because you are the best, and because you are the best it's normal that you are popular.* All of these books were accustomed to being fought over, to placing readers on waitlists, all of these books who were previously subjected to a rhythm of frenetic reading, with material degradation and premature aging as the cost of success, and now they were spending most of their time in the cool of the stacks. Except for one or two passing workers, they encountered no one.

The Popular Books discovered what it's like to be a book who is touched by only a handful of readers: the exclusion, the sidelining on the pretext of illegibility or irrelevance. They experienced unemployment interspersed with short assignments, a reader who takes you and reads you in two hours, and then nothing for weeks. They didn't understand what was happening to them, they couldn't believe what was being done to them. It was funny to watch. I had a good laugh at their misfortunes. In the evening, on the shelves, you could hear them whine: 'What's happening to us? Where are our faithful readers? What is our captive readership doing? What did we do to deserve this? It's not fair! It's not like we're poetry, dammit!'

During this time, the Affair continued to monopolize readers. Cruel and violent detective novels were all the rage. Deluged with hyperrealistic scenes of kidnapping and more and more detailed tales of torture, readers felt threatened. One of them had disappeared for real: he had believed he'd find refuge in books, and now books were torturing him. At the end of the day, it was the books who had captured the Historian. Who were keeping him as a prisoner. Who were inflicting on him the worst kinds of suffering.

From then on, readers believed reading could be dangerous. By opening a book, one ran the risk of being swallowed and turning up in some terrible place. Readers began to look at books with great distrust, especially those of literature, not only because they had ambiguous values, not always consistent with upholding the social order, but also because the safety of the reader was not guaranteed. They wrote to the Management.

Today, it is clear that the Books of Literature are unable to meet our expectations: they are serious when one wants to escape, they are whimsical and light when one needs to have serious answers. Too many seem self-centred, inaccessible, disconnected from reality, far removed from people's concerns. Between the sloppy books and the dense, the demagogic and the elitist, the moronic and the cerebral, the futile and the pretentious, it's difficult to find what one is looking for. We don't dispute that one small part of books remain intelligent and pleasant, but the heart of the problem is something else. The problem is that reading literature does not provide anything. No one can contest that: reading literature has never been an activity profitable in the short term. Even if it costs almost nothing, the fact is that reading yields very little. And it turns out that we now have to make our time profitable, even if it's time meant for leisure, that doesn't matter. This is probably the biggest change in recent years: now you have to know how to capitalize on everything, including your free time. We are not against the idea of reading without expecting something in return. We're simply saying that, given the current situation, we can no longer afford to engage in free activities. Reading without purpose, in a disinterested manner, without immediate benefit, we've already done it, we will still do it, but later, when we will have accomplished our goals, when we're stable and fulfilled, when we've succeeded and it's time for us to take a vacation. We ask that the library evolve to better meet our expectations. Today we need a library that is reactive, that allows for informing oneself, having fun, working, and seducing. We need a library that will let us anchor ourselves to the present, let us not miss a fantastic opportunity for career development, where we can respond directly to those job offers corresponding to our profile. We want a library that offers the possibility of increasing both our intellectual capacities and our power of seduction, of mobilizing us for noble causes, of accessing wealth, of enlarging our penises, and having efficient and cheap computer equipment. We want a library that allows us to change our lives, change our minds, change our dicks, change our jobs, that gives us the possibility of responding to the postings of our dreams in three clicks and of our soulmate in two. We want to change the course of our existence and learn to live in harmony with our environment. We want to both save the planet in the name of the common good and share our travel stories with the greatest possible number. We want to inform ourselves, distract ourselves, work, and all at the same time. We need a library that offers us the possibility of learning a foreign language in ten days, of writing a message of condolence that is modest and true. We need to be given the tools to compose a poem with emojis or a novel in two pages, to write an autobiography, to slip into a vampire's skin or imagine a steamy affair with our favourite star. We want to be able to give our opinions on the books and movies that are just coming out. We dream of writers, editors, animators, moderators, art critics, and being best friends with thousands of people. We need a library that furnishes us with the tools necessary to take our lives back into our own hands.

The readers had changed, their needs were different, and from then on they did just fine without books. Arriving in the Reading Room, they would switch on their computers and browse in search of who knows what – and for that matter they didn't seem to always know: things to look at, things to listen to. They were attached to the files they consumed rapidly and crazily, like they were opening thirty books at once. They started at Point A to get to Point Z; meanwhile, they sent the alphabet into disarray. By the time they arrived at Z, they had lost their initial goal, they'd forgotten what they'd come to look for, they'd forgotten the letter A, but at least they'd had a nice stroll, they'd taken pleasure in wandering into areas where they had never imagined going.

They moved from a cover letter to contesting an unreasonable fine, they followed up on an account of a voyage to an unknown land, a declaration of love, an insulting letter, a message of condolence, private jokes, a recipe, a practical joke, a rant, a manifesto, a contract, a deed of sale, a film critique, commercials, a book report, an edifying testimony. And too bad if these writings did not refer back to a real situation that would have had to be resolved, explained, clarified. The novel on which the report was based may not have been published, the testimonial might not not refer to anyone, the rejection letter may not respond to any application filed beforehand, and the so-called employer with the bizarre surname is not listed in any directory. As for the letters of condolence, which brought tears to your eyes and pushed some to reclaim the right to exercise justice with their own hands, as far back as the searches can go, there will be no trace of a death. That was the joke.

For access to networks of both false and true information, the readers, or at least those we have always called readers, imperatively needed a connection. This was the main request. You speak to them about the 14 million printed documents at their disposal, to remind them that a library is, to begin with, and above all, a collection, and they respond, *That's nice, this written heritage is remarkable, what a fabulous Treasure, we love being surrounded by books, and by the way, when will the internet connection be restored?*

In this new configuration, librarians did not have much to do other than sort out logistical questions. When they weren't being asked to fix the Wifi, they were being asked where the washrooms were. When they weren't being asked for directions to the washroom, they were asked to adjust the air conditioning. The readers are cold, turn up the heat; they're hot, counterbalance with cold air. The water fountain doesn't have any more cups? This chair needs to be replaced? Look at what their job has boiled down to. What does it have to do with the core of their trade? Absolutely nothing.

There was, nevertheless, a positive side to the situation. Because once the way to the washroom was known, once the water fountain was stocked with cups, once the internet was working and the temperature ideal, the librarians were finally left alone. And then they read. For the first time in their career, they were in a position to set aside a little bit of time to read at work.

But if they thought they'd be able to read peacefully, they were quite mistaken. There was no way to open a book without getting caught in the act.

As a book in the Great Library, I'd always considered the librarians if not friends then at least allies, and to see them put up with the presence of these readers who read only on their computers made me angry. The anger grew. I wrote to them to ask for an explanation:

Dear Librarians,

You can always congratulate yourselves on having a completely full Reading Room, but what do you know about those who occupy it? Who are they? Who discovered them? Of what evil spirit are they a creation? And what are they doing here? They're working, but still? What are they working on? And for who? Do they have a boss, or are they self-employed? Were they talked into coming, or did they come of their own accord? Are they here to defend any special interests? In that case, which ones? Is it enough to patronize the library to be considered a reader? How many readers are there in this room? Is that what we must continue to call those who visit? How do we recognize a reader when we see one?

You tell me that it isn't books who invented readers. It's true, that merit does not come back to us, no more than it comes back to the Library. There were readers before the Library opened. There will be readers after its demolition. They read before the first books were put into circulation, and they will continue to read after the publication of the last. The question isn't to know if they will continue to read, but what will they read, and how they will read: will they still read books, how many of us will survive, what will become of those the readers no longer want?

I demand answers.

Best regards,

The Angry Young Book

Upon reflection, the librarians said that yes, in fact, I wasn't wrong, the word *reader* had become inappropriate.

THE BLUE LIBRARIAN: Readers, that was before.

THE MAUVE LIBRARIAN: The word may have had its day.

THE WHITE LIBRARIAN: We should think about coming up with something else.

THE YELLOW LIBRARIAN: We need to have a meeting.

An urgent meeting is called.

The single item on today's agenda: defining the readers of today.

Six librarians discuss around a table.

THE GREEN LIBRARIAN: We could replace the term *readers* with *users*, it's more general.

THE BLUE LIBRARIAN: *Users, users*, why not.

THE RED LIBRARIAN: There's also the term *patrons* …

THE YELLOW LIBRARIAN: *Patrons*, no, that won't work, it's too … general.

Green and Blue agree. Red falls in with their opinion. When it comes down to it, she doesn't care any more than that about this proposition, she's proposed *patrons* to keep the discussion going.

THE WHITE LIBRARIAN: If neither *users* nor *patrons* work, we will have to invent a word.

THE MAUVE LIBRARIAN: Wait, I might have an idea. This new category of users is characterized by the fact that they sojourn in the room without really using the collections, don't you agree? So, in this case, I have a proposition: let's call them the *sojourners*.

Sojourner, noun – *S/he who takes advantage of the Reading Room by occupying a workstation without utilizing the Library's resources.* Syn. squatter.

I have known the Lectors, the scholars, the devotees, the fanatics, the skeptics. I've heard about those who read up close and those who read from afar. I knew that some people defined themselves as poachers, others as hikers, explorers, or wanderers. I thought I knew every type of reader, but I was wrong. I never saw the Sojourners coming. They were our poison. Right away I campaigned for them to be expelled or killed. Maybe not kill them, I said that out of anger, but at least force them out. I immediately requested that the obligation to read books be included in the rules and regulations. More precisely, I added four points:

1. Anyone entering the Reading Room is required to take a book and read it.
2. Anyone who refuses to borrow a book, or who is occupied only by the contents of their computer, will be immediately expelled by security.
3. Anyone expelled by security will be penalized with a temporary suspension of their library card for one week and the inability to access the Reading Room for an equivalent period of time.

4. If reprimanded three times, the offender will be permanently banned from the Great Library.

Rely on merciless rules of procedure. Impose coercive measures. Threaten and punish. Sanctions, it's unfortunate to say, are the only effective way. For me, it was war, war between the books and the non-readers. I was determined to lead. I wasn't afraid. I was ready to kill and even die to defend the cause.

I quickly understood that the librarians were not ready to die for the books. Despite their commitment to reading, they were not driven to this same extreme. It *was* a little excessive, and contrary to their concept of the profession. The Green Librarian argued that you could not expel someone from the Reading Room on the pretext that they were not reading.

'Once a person becomes a patron', she explained to me calmly, 'they cannot have their card taken away, except in the case of violence, a serious incident, the obvious degradation of property, or blatant theft. People come to the Library for good or bad reasons, but these reasons are theirs, we cannot contest them; as long as you do not disturb others, you can do what you want in the Reading Room, it's a very old principle, difficult to go back on. Don't worry, let the Sojourners have their phones and computers, it's temporary. One day they'll get bored and will return to the good old books they love … Besides, you need to stop overreacting! You cannot say that there is no one in the Reading Room: I will point out to you that we continue to welcome the Lectors. It's not much, we can agree on that, but there is still activity. Stop thinking that there is on one side the 'real readers' (silent, slow, solitary), and on the other side imposters (noisy, scattered, mobile). It's more complicated than that. Books change, libraries change, and there's no reason for the readers not to change. I totally agree with you, we live in troubled times, we don't really know where we stand, but in my opinion, it won't last, one day new readers will come.' (She said these last words in a very soft voice, giving me a small pat on the cover as if to say *don't worry, it'll all work out*.)

'If you say so,' I responded, without conviction, 'we'll see.'

Thus I awaited the return of the real readers. I was skeptical. I observed very closely.

In terms of attendance, the spring came up empty. The traditional increase due to terrified students in the lead-up to exams did not take place this year. The students preferred to work at home, one eye on their work, the other on the broadcast of a famous tennis tournament, and so what if in the end their attention was grabbed by the victory of a young Spaniard in three sets at the expense of three essays by an old Austrian on the theory of sexuality.

The summer months made it possible to welcome a wider audience. It's not that in the summer citizens are overcome by an irrepressible desire to read, but, since its entry into the rank of Heritage Masterpiece, the Great Library welcomes tourists. The chance to *revitalize the relationship with the public*, according to the terms chosen by the Communications Department.

Led by a guide with a low voice, the tourists swooned before the collections' richness, all of these treasures, all of this information, this heritage, all of this knowledge, 14 million volumes which, you realize, would take 150,000 years to read. The tourists loved the visit, but not to the point of hampering themselves with reading works of visual poetry, religious anthropology, or industrial archaeology.

At the end of the paid visit, each visitor was issued a new-generation Library Card. An idea from Communications: take advantage of these visits by launching cards intended for tourists. Restricted access to collections (two documents per month). The possibility of personalizing your card with, you choose, four images from the Treasure (a page from a precious manuscript, an old master print, an antique map, an autograph).

The card issued to tourists was designed to be less plain than the Researcher Card. A card that's more pretty than useful, critiqued some. To which it was replied that access to knowledge had nothing to gain from an austere presentation. Well, come on, I'll admit these cards were rather pretty, provided we admit that their results weren't good. The summertime visitors didn't use these pretty cards. Not for borrowing books, in any case. They kept them, of course, as souvenirs from their travels. Imperishable souvenirs to set before their eyes each day, to see before each meal and even in between meals. Because Communications had designed a card on magnetic material so that, for those who would not use it, they could, rather than throw it away, stick it on the door of the fridge. And with every craving, they would remember the Great Library's existence. A Library Card that is also a fridge magnet: a bit of marketing genius applied to library science.

In the end, a lot more marketing, and still fewer readers.

In the middle of the night, ghosts entered the Library through the third basement. Once in the stacks, they pulled the slow-moving books (fewer than five consultations in the last two years) to pack them in crates. The ghosts were actually individual contractors, disguised at the Library's expense. They were paid by volume: each Slow-Moving Book pulled from the shelves earned them a certain amount of money. Incredibly motivated, conscientious, methodical, in relation to their miserable wages. Their poor pay did not slow them; they demonstrated a terrifying efficiency. Under the knowing eye of the surveillance cameras, they were committing the unforgivable.

The Slow-Moving Books removed from the shelves had been erased from the catalogues and sent to a place from which one never returned: the pulper.

When I called him to account, the Director of Collections got on his high horse and claimed I didn't understand the process. Although he acknowledged that individual contractors had indeed been hired to do some weeding, he refuted the fact that they were there to *assassinate the books*, as I had remarked to him. He found the expression misleading. He threatened to sue me and have me censored if I repeated my attack.

'This has nothing to do with assassination,' he said, 'but with updating the collections. I'm sorry to tell you, but you're not using the right words, you've got the wrong vocabulary.'

'I'm using the right words,' I retorted, 'and we do indeed have a disagreement about vocabulary, meaning a disagreement about the facts. You have most certainly set up a program for the elimination of books. You can't deny it. To me, you are an assassin.'

The Director of Collections chuckled. I realized he was going to lecture me.

'Listen, our goal isn't to eliminate but to add value to our collections. As the heritage library, it would be against our mission to eliminate documents. We aren't savages, we work according to intellectual and material criteria, scientific criteria known to all. Our work is perfectly clear and transparent. Our documents policy obeys a charter I invite you to consult. In general, we are moving toward increasing our collections, even though it's true that some works are eliminated. So, yes, we have some loss, but it's marginal. And know that the Slow-Moving Books do not go to the pulper. They go to join a warehouse, or they're redirected to a more suitable library. In any case, they will be kept and available for anyone who requests them.'

Impossible to speak with this guy. He doesn't care about the truth. The only thing that interests him is always being right. So I let him talk. But I didn't believe for a second this version of the facts. To me, he was messing with reality.

Deep down, what he really wanted was to get rid of the weaker ones among us. And I knew it was just the beginning. First they went after books that hadn't been read in over a decade, then they took the others. The young books like me were condemned to death.

I had to do something. I thought the best thing would be to put the library in disorder. I talked about it with the books I was closest to. All found the idea interesting, and they agreed to help carry it out. So all those who felt in danger moved from one shelf to another. None of them were lost, simply out of place. For example, the work listed as 8' KD 12225 had taken the place of 8' KE 12225 – and vice versa. Slight disruptions that prevented the contractors from getting their hands on Slow-Moving Books: they were never where they were supposed to be.

Unfortunately, this penalized the Library's last readers, the Lectors. When a Lector asked for a book, every second time he received a notice bearing the word *disappeared*. We knew perfectly well we were putting the establishment in danger: nothing is worse, for a library, than to have its collections in disorder. But did we have any other solutions?

To counteract our actions, the contractors received help from the library clerks, who were granted a special bonus by the Management for this additional work. The Slow-Moving Books who had changed places were found.

Looking for another way to fight, I came up with a second level of disorder, more radical, more complex: this time it was about completely changing towers.

Books belonging in the Tower of Novels were thus found in that of Heritage.

The Unclassifiables went to hide in the Tower of Sciences and Humanities.

Some disciplines intermixed: art got close to the social sciences, history flirted with contemporary literature, experimental poetry fucked political economy in the ass.

Seeing as the Director of Collections still refused to hear me, I modified the catalogue. With the help of a Librarian, I amused myself by introducing unknown subjects, I invented categories and genres.

The category *Contemporary Novels* wound up divided into sub-categories:

Written directly on a computer
Written first by hand
Annotated
Has the words *red* or *blue* in the title
Has the words *yellow* or *white* in the title
Whose gender is uncertain
Noisy
Inoffensive
Bad-tempered
Lukewarm
Annoying
Who will go ignored
Who will go from hand to hand

The Library was completely disorganized. The Lectors complained to the higher powers that it was practically impossible to get their hands on a book. This information moved up to the Minister of Knowledge and the Dissemination of Information, who spoke to the Director of Collections, who was not very happy:

'Listen, this situation cannot go on any longer. Put the Library back in order. Agree to the books' requests. Throw out these Sojourners! Or it's me who you're going to throw out. And publish a press release. Now.'

Aware of the dangers weighing on the institution, the Management of the Great Library has decided, in agreement with the Board of Directors and the Scientific Committee, and with the guidance of the Minister of Knowledge and Dissemination of Information, to revive an ambitious policy in support of books. As such, *the obligation for users to read a monograph or an issue of a periodical upon each visit to the Reading Room* is from this point forward listed in the Rules of Procedure. The Management formally commits to proposing a policy adhering to that of today's public reading establishment: responding to new expectations and new uses, all while developing and enhancing its own funds.

Despite the injunction, the Sojourners refused to give in to the requirement to read printed materials. They were shut out of the Library. But in shutting them out, the Reading Room was emptied. The Library saw a record drop in attendance: 90 percent less than the same time the year before. Now the room is deserted. You don't believe me? Look up and see for yourself.

The Red
Librarian

I was reading at the circulation desk, I had the book well in hand when I felt it start getting warm. I barely had the chance to say to myself, *Hm, this book is hot,* when it became burning hot, and I had to drop it. Falling about twenty centimetres, it landed on the glass, aluminum, and glossy laminate surface. In the moment, I was afraid it'd been hurt. I called out to it: it responded to its name. I examined it: nothing broken. This Angry Young Book was sturdier than I'd thought.

I recommended he take a rest and carefully closed him. After sitting for such a long time, I needed to stretch my legs. I went to take a walk around the Reading Room.

Behind the glass panels, the wind had picked up, the clouds were moving at a speed perceptible to the naked eye. The sun peeked out between two clouds and the rays of light engulfed a Reading Room that now seemed to me bigger than usual.

The walls seemed to have been pushed back, the work-spaces enlarged, the open-access shelves resized. But don't get me wrong: it was the absence of the public that gave this impression.

To reduce the feeling of emptiness, the space had been divided into eight medium-sized squares – the work of an ergonomic designer who had come to see the room a few weeks earlier. Upon delivering his conclusions, he stated that it was necessary to densify. At first he used the verb *densify*, which in this context sounded rather nice. He followed up with the word *streamline*, which sounded even better. The ergonomic designer must have felt he hit the nail on the head, because he insisted on the necessity to *streamline the space*. The expression greatly pleased Management, who immediately decided to give him the means to carry it out.

Once the space had been streamlined, a sign was put up informing readers that they were henceforth invited to take a spot in the squares located near the main entrance. They were told that the back of the room was still accessible, but they should know this section was lit only by daylight and that the heat back there had been turned down – an agreement having been reached that there was no use in heating walls and there were absolutely more important things to do than light an empty space.

Returning to my post at the welcome desk, I found the Angry Young Book asleep on the table. Judging from its sober, almost neutral cover, it seemed calm, even nice. Like one of those brave little books that coax their reader. There were no indications that this thin, seemingly innocuous volume was nervous and anxious, prey to nightmares that made it sick. That caused me pain. I studied it closely, it breathed softly, I whispered:

'It's me, the Red Librarian. I would like to tell you something. I think you're a good book. Thanks to you, I've learned many things. I will tell my friends about you. I will say to them, *Read it, you won't regret it.'*

I put my hand on the cover again. Its temperature had gone down. Reassured it was better, I reopened it.

I was at the part where the characters delicately place a foot on a velvet carpet. Could they be trying to enter a place without being spotted by the person at reception? That's what we were soon going to find out.

While reading, I began to hear the sound of footsteps muffled by a carpet playing accomplice. I thought I recognized the swishing of loafers and the creaking of derby shoes. I positively identified the sound of Oxfords, the sort of wheezing the leather makes when the foot enters the thrust phase. For me, in this moment, there was no doubt that readers had just entered the Reading Room and, step by step, were approaching me. Readers sporting loafers or derby shoes – to my knowledge there weren't quite fifty of them, these last readers of the Library, the last of the faithful, those who go by the name Lectors.

The Lectors: in other words, the persons of letters, the scholars, the academic readers. They practice the profession of teacher-researchers, teacher-writers, even writer-researchers. Great familiarity with institutions of knowledge. Eminent members of the Library. They deserve to be decorated for their attendance. They've been here for so long it feels like they've always been here. It's said about them, for laughs, *they're part of the furniture.* The immobility implied in this expression, *part of the furniture*, must not mislead us. The Lectors have always been active. They borrow books, they suggest purchases, they offer their own publications, they fully participate in the life of the establishment. The Library is an absolutely essential resource in successfully completing their research. They use it to nourish their teachings and, not insignificantly, as a place of informal exchange with their colleagues.

One thing surprised me. Usually the Lectors would arrive rather late in the morning, rarely before 11 a.m., preferably later, between noon and two, or even in the middle of the afternoon. Now, for the first time in their careers, they were morning people.

'Ma'am?'

Ma'am? I knew this voice. It was the voice of Work. Work often spoke to me in this honeyed-yet-authoritarian tone, part of its charm. It'd come to remind me of my duties. It'd call me to order. It meant I must perform the tasks for which I was responsible to earn my salary and social recognition. It didn't tell me outright, but it wanted me to put down my book to get back to it right away. I didn't want to give in. The Angry Young Book had made me combative.

'Excuse me, ma'am.'

As Work insisted, I stated, without raising my eyes from my book, that, doing my duties, I was busy, and until retirement. I added that I had an excellent service record. Since the beginning of my career, my superiors had been satisfied. You could check. I wasn't given these promotions for nothing. And (in parentheses) I still had thirty years of working full-time before I could retire. One hundred and twenty trimesters in a Reading Room, did it have any idea what all of that means? And here I asked for a small minute of freedom, enough time to finish my chapter, and Work reproached me!

'Ma'am, don't take it personally.'

One minute of reading for oneself out of thirty years working full-time, it was a negligible quantity, it didn't even count. Then I would greet the Lectors. I would respond to their expectations. I would help them with their research, if that was what they wanted. I would create bibliographies, if that was what pleased them. I would go get them journal articles myself, if it made them happy. They would understand what it was like to work with the Red Librarian.

'Ma'am, we aren't in a hurry, we can wait, finish your chapter.'

'I'm yours, I'm all yours in a second. Just a second.'

So I put down my book, and I straightened up.

To my great surprise, I found myself facing a group of strangers. Ten or so young people sporting loafers, Oxfords, derby shoes, but dressed like no one else. Although the room is heated, they hadn't bothered to remove their huge parkas; they'd only agreed to take their hands out of their pockets to pull back their hoods, under which they wore elf hats, bucket hats, and caps flanked with mysterious slogans as if they were paid to promote a drink sold in another galaxy.

Judging by how organized they were, they hadn't just come in because the weather was bad or the air icy, or because the really short days encouraged being inside an enclosed and temperate space. Everything led me to believe that they had pushed open the door of the Library with the aim of becoming readers. They seemed sure of themselves, prepared, convinced, determined to become patrons of the establishment. With a practiced gesture, they pulled already completed registration forms out of their pockets. They handed me proof of residence and identification. All the required pieces were there, nothing was missing, the applications were complete, and right the first time, if you can believe it. And to top it all off, they each presented a contract.

'A contract?'

It was certainly the first time in my career I'd seen readers' contracts. At first I thought they were fake. However, by examining the documents more closely, then telephoning the Director of Collections for confirmation, I saw that it was precisely that: these young people had gotten jobs at the Library as Contractual Readers.

'Very well,' I said. 'We are colleagues, in a way. Welcome.'

Once registered, the Contractual Readers went to find spots, which they easily found. After which they unpacked their things, connected their laptops to the Library network, and ordered books. While waiting for them to be delivered, they went to the vending machine. In the uncomfortable space of the cafeteria, they drank their teas and coffees. Ten minutes later, they came to retrieve their documents from the circulation desk and went back to their spots. Books in hand, they went to work.

Over the course of the morning, a second wave arrived, followed by a third, then a fourth, and again a fifth, it didn't stop. An unthinkable thing in the last months: a queue formed in the hall.

Two hours after opening, the room was three-quarters full. It was filled with Contractuals.

An hour later, it was full. Not a single free spot.

Twelve-thirty. Ah, here are the Lectors.

Lost in their thoughts, some greet me, while others abstain, no doubt judging this effort pointless; still others don't ask themselves this question or even know what we're talking about. Some will see me ten thousand times and still always be incapable of recognizing me. On top of moving slowly and daydreaming, the Lectors suffer from near-sightedness. It is no doubt because of this they need a moment before seeing that, this morning, the room is in fact full.

'The Reading Room is full, how is this so?' asked one of them, astonished.

Seeing the expression on his face, I understood that he had never been faced with this predicament; in fact he had never heard this sentence. It should be noted that, since the Sojourners left, the Reading Room belonged to the Lectors. They tended to think of themselves as being at home in the Library. They were comfortable here. It may no longer have been the meeting place they knew and loved, but at least they were sure to find a spot whatever their arrival time. It suited them well, considering they'd never really had schedules. They always came when they felt like it, between two seminars, before a colloquium; they came to look for resources, to meet with a colleague or speak with a student. In the past, in the days of large crowds, I recall having seen very young readers give up their barely warmed seats so that a Lector could sit there. Which leads me to believe that the magisterium exercised by the Lectors is not merely intellectual, but also includes an aspect of real estate.

'Full, but in what way?' the Lector asked me again, proof he'd understood absolutely nothing.

'The room's capacity is not unlimited,' I argued. 'Registration is on the rise, now it's first-come-first-served. To make sure you have a place to sit, you must come a lot earlier, 9:20, 9:30 at the latest.'

The next day, the Lectors once again arrived late morning/early afternoon.

The following days, same thing, 11:30, noon, 1:00 – there wasn't much to be done, this had always been their time slot. Readers' habits can't be changed just like that.

I kept telling them that from 9:20, 9:30 on, it was over, you have to assume all the spots will be taken.

'Understood, dear lady,' they responded, 'it slipped my mind, but it's OK, this time I'm keeping the information firmly in mind, I'll speak to my colleagues, starting tomorrow we will arrive earlier.'

Incorrigible and impossible, they continued to show up far too late. And I, good natured, spent my time explaining and re-explaining the situation, I repeated the same thing a hundred times, I spoke to them like children. I couldn't take it anymore.

Even if I didn't mean a word of it, I commiserated.

'I'm truly sorry.'

'Don't say you're sorry,' snapped the Dean of the Lectors, 'don't be afraid of the truth. There is no longer any space for us here. This may not be what you wanted, but it's a fact, an indisputable fact. We've well understood where you are heading, you're in the process of kicking us out.'

For lack of places to sit, the Lectors ended up going home, dragging their feet. They complained. They really weren't happy. On the way, their discontent turned to sadness. They were heartbroken about being rejected from the establishment they had frequented for so long, to the point of having been considered *part of the furniture*. It was a part of their cultural memory, even their lives, that was going away. Like an old friend who turns his back on you after making it clear that you are no longer friends. And who, as you approach the door, yells: *And don't you ever come back!*

They were quite a sight, these Contractual Readers. As they arrived in small groups, seemingly independent of each other, I didn't notice right away the overall unity. When I realized it, I saw they had given the Reading Room an unusual colouring; they'd imposed their rhythm, their style, their ways of doing things.

In their appearances, they dared absurd combinations: navy double-breasted blazer with white butcher pants and white loafers/fleece jacket with velour pants and tasselled loafers/Chesterfield coat with boxing shorts, tights, and heeled Oxfords.

They weren't afraid to mix two styles, the academic and the sporty, a way of showing they considered reading to be at the same time a science, an art, and a sport, an intellectual activity and a physical challenge.

Some Contractuals brought back elements that were thought to have been lost forever: a smock with sparkly leather epaulettes, a blood-red vinyl jacket with batwing sleeves.

So many pieces I never thought to reappear, especially on the bodies of readers.

Unlike the scholars and the savants, the group of Lectors on whom everything was new or like new, the

Contractuals wore ripped jackets, misshapen trousers, buttonless shirts.

They paired traditional scholarly clothing (gabardine, blazer, velour, loafers) with items that seemed to have been picked at random from thrift store bins or bought for next to nothing at a flea market.

On some pieces, the topstitching remained visible or the tacking thread hadn't been removed – the clothes looked like they were still being made.

They had a distinct way of wearing their Oxfords, derby shoes, and loafers. You can't say they wore them, more so that they slipped them on like slippers, crushing the backs with their heels. I came to realize why they didn't put the entirety of their feet inside the shoes: the size of their shoes didn't match the size of their feet. And so these rather chic city shoes were were being treated like sandals, slippers, or flipflops. Originally social, urban, active, serious, professional footwear, Oxfords, derby shoes, and loafers had a change in status: they became examples of pleasure, associated with leisure, unemployment, free time – shoes ideal for a quiet afternoon at the 'Lib.'

At the same time, I had a hard time believing the Contractuals had bought these shoes. No one, in my opinion, is twisted enough to knowingly get the wrong size. I asked myself if the Contractuals had not stripped the Lectors of their academic uniforms to combine them with poorer elements, in the manner of pirates marrying elegant stolen frock coats with their own capri pants and stolen shapeless trousers. Perhaps the Contractuals were trying to get a message across: they wouldn't be so much new readers as new Lectors, their hidden daughters and sons, degenerate forms of readers, bastards, mutants.

While the Lectors had popularized the wearing of corrective lenses, the Contractuals were equipped with lightweight headphones, enveloping, fashionable, with or without a cord. Some preferred in-ear earbuds, with a silicone or foam end-piece that was lodged into the ear canal. To listen to sound without troubling the tranquility of the Reading Room, they had invested in new and powerful listening devices.

Headphones over their ears and heads full of sound, they weren't hearing, they weren't speaking, they were listening to their soundtracks. Which did not prevent them from wearing, in addition to their headphones, Smart Glasses with a titanium frame and a small screen hanging in the corner of the lens, which recorded things seen, things read, then sent the result of their readings to a remote storage space.

To provide a complete picture of the Contractuals, I must add they were equipped with thermoses filled with coffee or tea, alternating their consumption with sips of energy drinks. At regular intervals, they nibbled dried fruits, crunched cereal bars, chewed on bananas, and gulped down yogurts. At noon and in the evening, they ate raw vegetables and pasta in sauce. They ate their meals directly from the clear plastic boxes that allowed their preservation.

They seemed to follow a diet comparable to that of athletes getting ready to make a sustained and lengthy effort that required them to build up energy reserves to draw on until the end.

At the time I didn't know what conclusion to draw except that with all that in their stomachs, they must be extremely tough, capable of maintaining a high rhythm of work over a long period. With this long-distance-runner diet, I deduced they were preparing for a long and intense stay in the Reading Room.

Even more than their looks, what stood out about the Contractuals was their pace of working.

For the Contractuals, money was time, and time must be converted into reading.

There was a minimum of ten books per person per day, which was almost one book per hour, and at this pace for seven days a week.

From a librarian's recollection, I've never seen such fast readers. Throughout my career, I've known some characters. I've seen them, crazies, in the Reading Room. I've met maniacs and madmen, I've done business with Mrs. and Mr. Know-It-Alls, I've met scholars, hung out with living encyclopedias. But like that, never. The Contractuals read ultra-fast, and in very large quantities. Where others would have spent days, a few hours were enough for them to say, about an enormous language dictionary: 'Read it! On to the next!'

They went through monstrous volumes with great speed. They devoured dictionaries, swallowed encyclopedias, gobbled tons of directories, stacks of catalogues, metres and metres of bibliographies.

Swift and determined readers, they turned the pages at a regulated pace. Reading did not procure in them any emotion. Stone-faced, no bursts of laughter or shedding of tears, no expressions of boredom, signs of irritation, nor apparent enthusiasm or pleasure.

Smart Glasses perched on their noses, they were as expressive as a scanner snapping a book. In front of an opened book, their eyes brightened; when the book closed, their pupils darkened. With the aid of a backlighting system, they modified at leisure the pages' brightness, improving the legibility by accentuating the contrast between the white spaces and the printed characters.

They worked with headphones over their ears, nodding their heads, which occasionally led them to abandon their mechanical gestures to suddenly raise an arm and move it in time. But to what were they dancing? This soundtrack that accompanied them, was it that of books? Or were they listening to sounds coming from outside, wind, rain, traffic, music, bells, screams, sirens?

Quantity took precedence. It was about reading fast and a lot, no matter the content. Whether they stumbled upon a reference by tapping basic terms into the search index, or were suggested recommendations – *If you like this, you'll also love* – each title seemed to have been pulled from the collections more or less at random; more precisely, none seemed to be a matter of choice. An individual was in possession of a thesaurus, but they might as well have had the Encyclopedia of Islam; nothing led me to think that the book in their hands responded to a thirst for knowledge, or that they were there to derive pleasure. They went from one text to the next with indifference, as if responding to a type of sporting challenge. I had, above all, the feeling I was witnessing a competition where only the participants knew the rules.

The Library Clerks were the first to notice when the arbitrary nature of these readings gave way to a rigorous, almost military-like organization. Because they processed the orders, they ended up noticing that no title was requested twice, no book was subjected to a second consultation. Despite the large number of requests, none were related to the same title, which meant that the Contractuals were coordinated, they were working as a team. With the goal of scanning every text? To go through the entirety of knowledge?

At some point, it became clear the Contractuals were dividing up the collections: they had formed teams, each team in charge of a portion of the works. After having scanned the reference books, they attacked the monographs.

The biggest group, in number of readers, bore the title Community.

The Community was devoted solely to Literature.

The Literature Community was subdivided into ten Sub-Communities:

• the first Sub-Community went through Novels: National, Regional, Small Town, Suburban, Urban, Stateless;

• the second took care of Novels to Read on the Train, to Read at Home, Comfortably in an Armchair, to Read in a Hospital Bed;

• the third tackled the group of Inoffensive Novels, the series of Novels That Make You Feel Good, not forgetting the coalition of Super Nice Novels;

• the fourth swept through Novels of the Past, the Present, and Novels for the Future;

• the fifth undertook the Athletic Sagas, Technological Fables, Alternate Histories, Fan Novels, Novels with Police and Vampires;

• the sixth had the heavy burden of reading the Emotionally Disturbed, On Edge, Raving Mad Novels;

• the seventh plunged into the Big Novels, a generic term grouping various things like the Large Epics, the Sturdy and Verbose, the Complete Autobiographies, Genealogical Novels, and Interminable Series;

• the eighth explored the realm of Poetry and Lyrics;

• the ninth approached Literary Theory;

• and, last, the tenth Sub-Community took interest in the books that had escaped the previous nine, mostly declassified, badly classified, not-easy-to-classify works: bastard types, intermediary novels, works of wild theory.

It is my understanding that the members of the Community suffered from having to process such a massive array. The number of novels in the Library's collections was such that they believed they would never reach the end, the fault of a birthrate that remains extremely high within the realm of fiction. No time to finish one while ten others are born: it's a direct consequence of the 'new releases' phenomenon, which governs production in the area. And as if it weren't enough that heaps of novels are born each day, there are other books that have ended up, involuntarily, classified among the novels. They were put in this category on the pretext that they had the potential to bring back to the novel readers who had distanced themselves from it, having judged it obsolete, outdated, extinct (these books were reviving literature, it was said, insofar as they worked on behalf of the novel). In short, between those who considered themselves novels and those who found themselves involuntarily associated, the number of novels to process was considerable, a genuine bottomless pit.

Nevertheless, the work was done, the mission was carried out, and even if it seemed like all of the novels didn't exactly *read like novels*, each was perfectly scanned. I pay homage here to the courage and perseverance demonstrated by the Community of Readers of Literature.

A second group, called Division, was in charge of the Sciences and Humanities.

The Division decided to divide the collections not according to disciplines, but by the research theme.

Of them, there are seven. A result of which, seven Sub-Divisions were created:

• the first Sub-Division read all that was relevant to the theme 'Networked Society';

- the second Sub-Division took charge of works related to the theme 'Territories, Movements, Inequalities';
- the third was devoted to 'Conflicts and Competitions';
- the fourth reviewed papers on the theme 'Ethics and Finance';
- the fifth examined with much seriousness 'Employment and Violence';
- the sixth devoured everything related to 'Health and Immortality';
- the seventh finished the job by not missing anything devoted to 'Creative Hobbies and Personal Development.'

The flawless organization of the Division into seven Sub-Divisions made it so that the work was a little bit boring, but overall effective. For this rigorous, well-done job, I offer my congratulations to the Division of Sciences and Humanities.

The third reading group was nothing to do with a groupuscule, yet this is the name that it chose.

The Groupuscule had the difficult task of reading the Unclassifiables.

Its structure was less rigid than that of the Community and the Division. This corresponded to the profound nature of the Unclassifiables, which have always refused to belong to any school of thought, do not recognize the division of knowledge into disciplines, and ignore the question of genre. There was even a Sub-Groupuscule assigned to the 'sick,' and another to the 'demented' – although the dividing line between these and the so-called 'normal' was completely arbitrary – but for the rest, each member of the Groupuscule remained free to choose their documents. It was sufficient to help oneself and mention the *reads* on the Great Register of Readings.

It was nice, I thought, to work in the Groupuscule. They were relaxed, they didn't forbid themselves from laughing, but, mind you, they still worked, they laughed while working. Good work, you see, despite some deviations at the behavioural level, particularly regular breaches of the required silence in the room.

There were few cool names left when the fourth group was formed.

After the members came together, they decided to unite under the banner Squad.

The Squad was dedicated to the reading of rare and heritage collections:

- first Sub-Squad: manuscripts;
- Second Sub-Squad: letters;
- Third Sub-Squad: handwritten documents.

Not much to report concerning the work within the group, other than that the ancient Heritage books were by far the least numerous, so the Squad was quickly done with them.

Its members were consequently reassigned to the other three teams. The luckiest went to giggle with the Unclassifiables. One part worked in the Sciences and Humanities group. The last went to reinforce the troops in the Literature Community. Interminable Series, Complete Autobiographies, and Genealogical Novels were on the program. Stories whose length did not meet a need but seemed to fall under a predatory logic. It sometimes seemed it was about capturing the reader's attention to make sure they no longer had the energy nor the time to dedicate to competing books:

• total and infinite history of a magical realm in perpetual conflict, constant adventures, inextricable plots, complicated love, murders that demand revenge;

• my complete life in twenty volumes, 6,000 hyperdetailed pages in which we learn that daily life is a struggle;

• etc.

From having watched them at length, I can say that the Contractual Readers have been useful, determined, efficient, responsible, competent, organized, invested, and serious agents. Completely devoted to their mission, they gave themselves completely over to that for which they were paid. Not the kind to daydream with their noses in the air, they worked without stopping. Their concentration was rarely found to be wanting. Nothing seemed able to distract them from the work they carried out morning to night, Monday to Monday, day and night combined.

Respectful of their schedules, they waited for their break to get some air in the garden (open only for strolls), or even to do fifteen minutes of exercise in the fitness centre. When fatigue began to set in, they allowed themselves a moment of rest by stretching out on one of the cots placed at their disposal. Fifteen minutes of napping from which they returned fresh and ready to see the job through.

From start to finish, they demonstrated good teamwork, they were seen helping, encouraging one another. The result was the idea that a Contractual Reader could always count on one of his colleagues in times of hardship, fatigue, weariness, sickness. Whatever the circumstances, their professionalism never faltered, which is all the stronger considering they are originally not of the profession.

From the beginning they showed themselves to be quick and efficient. I was convinced they had gone out too fast, that they would be unable to keep up the pace. They were going to tire. Exhausted, they would slow down. Yet, not at all, they always read faster, as if from day to day they increased their abilities, as if their minds were ever more powerful. Between the start and end of their contract, I got the impression their heads had doubled in size.

And yet, it can't be said that the task was easy. Day and night, repeating this same movement consisting of taking a physical book, one of those printed ones, which they opened and scanned with their glasses. And so on, page after page, volume after volume, night after night, for the entirety of the printed materials, this was their mission, their commitment, their work, their prison.

To think that there are some who still believe people don't work at libraries! The Contractual Readers could bear witness to the contrary. To hear tell, on the day the contracts were signed, the Director of Collections greedily exclaimed: 'Thank God, work certainly isn't what's missing here!' At the time, the Contractuals hadn't taken this sentence seriously. They wondered what God had to do with it before understanding, a little late, that the most important word in the sentence was *work*; in the hierarchy, God came second.

The Contractuals were very quickly able to identify, and resolve, problems that arose for them, whether they were technical points or issues related to the organization of the chain of work. During periods of great stress, when Management ordered them to produce more, they demonstrated an increased efficiency, without ever losing their composure.

The work of digitizing all the collections had to be done in a very short time frame because some books were not well. Sick, vulnerable, weakened, depressed, anxious, their conditions noticeably deteriorated. Despite stable environmental conditions, controlled humidity and temperature, mould was developing on their printed pages. The presence of these micro-organisms, which took the form of light or dark stains, attracted psocoptera, a type of book lice, which came to feed on them. Cockroaches, moths, woodworms, and rodents would start nibbling on the paper, leather, parchment. The old books, according to Senior Management, were in great danger. For lack of being able to fight against these degradations, it was urgent to make backup copies.

To serve the Contractuals, the Library Clerks were forced into an infernal rhythm. Which went fast, too fast. They finished the week worn out, crushed by the workload, in a state of muscular fatigue comparable to that of a runner who has calculated his effort to run exactly 42.195 km and who, unable to run a single metre more, collapses while crossing the finish line. I know there have been multiple injuries among the staff. Three quarters come from stress fractures, occupational accidents quite unprecedented in the history of reading.

One fine morning, a book no one was expecting suddenly appeared in the Reading Room. Softcover, unluxurious paper, dubious inking, a cheaply produced booklet, a small book without qualities, a fragile object, however tough-nosed. With its damaged cover, it looks older than its age. I would have said nineteen, twenty years old, when it is hardly even ten.

According to the numbers I have, one hundred and twenty people have read it in its entirety; between two and three hundred were satisfied with leafing through it. A very few know only that it exists – poor book, you can't say that it's had an easy life. From an early age, it has suffered mistreatment. Brutes with dirty fingers have handled it with no regard for its physical integrity. They turned the pages between their thumb and index finger, as if it were a flip book, any old thing. They've left it in a pitiful state, cover creased, pages dog-eared. I'm not certain they would have dared to do the same with one of the Classic Books, the cowards. Although it dreamt neither of success or fame, the Small Wounded Book had not expected such treatment. It still hoped to receive a bit of consideration.

It needs to be said that this little book has a disadvantage: it, who belongs to no genre, was born in a great period of novelistic hegemony, at the worst time, right in the middle of novel season, just at the end of summer, when readers return from vacation hungry for something new and are told with aplomb: *if you want something new, these are the novels, come discover our selection.*

When the Small Wounded Book came out in bookstores, when it made its entrance into the collections of public libraries, when it appeared in the world of reading, novels monopolized the readers to the point that there was no longer space for other species, judged deviant.

The Small Wounded Book tried to hide its difference by passing as a novel; this was not a bad idea, far from it, it was a good move. Alas, the manoeuvre didn't work: bookstores and libraries didn't fall for it, they placed it among the Unclassifiables. Once wedged into these shelves where few people venture, between two young but already dusty volumes, the Small Wounded Book faded from memory. It thought itself condemned to a perpetuity without readers until one fine morning a Contractual Reader took it in his hands, and, quite unexpectedly, lingered on the text.

That morning, a Contractual looked for a long time at the cover, which he found beautiful and pleasant to the touch. He liked this title, *The Small Wounded Book.* Intrigued, he opened the volume. Contravening his mission, he did not just scan it, he began to slowly read it. He claimed ownership of it to the point of calling it *my book.* At break, he took his book with him; he continued to read it while drinking a coffee. When one of his colleagues greeted him with a tap on the shoulder, he barely responded, he cut the communication short with a gesture that meant both *hi* and *leave me alone*. He didn't want to waste time chatting. Only his book was of any importance, and anything that infringed upon the reading of his book was an aggression, a nuisance. For nothing in the world would he have wanted to skip a sentence. This book deserved him devoting all of his attention to it.

Every now and then he took a break from reading, lifted his nose, allowed himself a few seconds of reflection, and plunged back into the text.

Our reader ended up losing all track of time, perhaps not of time in general but in any case productive time, to the point of forgetting to return to his post at the appointed time (if he were to have been told that Work was calling him back to order, he would have curtly replied, *later*). He had better things to do, more interesting, more useful.

The legal break time was pretty much over, yet the Contractual still had not returned to work. Despite having read his book through to the end, he went back to taste another paragraph, a chapter, a sentence, to postpone the moment when he would have to separate from it. He was already dying to read it again. And for that matter, he would have willingly kept it under his elbow, if others had not already called for it. Some had expressed their desire for the Small Wounded Book to become theirs, even for a day or two.

All it took was for one Contractual Reader to appear to enjoy a book for others in turn to want it. The Small Wounded Book, of which the Library possessed only one copy, became in a few days the object of many desires. Two days earlier it had been of interest to no one, and now almost all of the Contractuals wanted to find out about it, to know what was inside it, what it said, what experience it offered – and the sooner the better.

I even attempted, in my role as a librarian, to calm the Contractuals by offering them another book as a substitute, but that didn't work. It's my fault. I don't know what came over me to offer them books from the 'That Make You Feel Good' list. Very bad idea. The first person to read one hated it. He hadn't even gotten to the bottom of page 8 when the book fell from his hands. He wanted to persevere, but as he progressed, he was beset by a growing exasperation, I heard him exhale loudly, audibly agitated; he was belching, snickering. After twenty pages, his eyes were bulging, hand trembling, sweat beading on his forehead as if he were possessed. I even thought he was going to physically attack the Feel-Good Book. I pictured the moment when he was going to rip out the pages and tear off the cover. In order to prevent this massacre, I went to ask him what was wrong. I addressed him in a voice both soft and conciliatory.

'Is something wrong?'

Fixating me with his wild eyes, the guy declared:

'I'm sorry to tell you but this thing does not belong here. I asked you for a book and you gave me a non-book.

Have you at least read it? No? Ah, well, I'm going to give you the pitch: it's the story of a book that, given the choice, would have preferred to be a film or a television series. It's the story of a book who offers to visualize the film that it could be and will be if an opportunity for adaptation arises. It's a book who is a book by default, for the time being, for lack of anything better. It's a book who doesn't like books too much. My opinion: a reading experience worthy of a TV program. Stop me if I'm mistaken, but I've heard it said that certain public reading establishments have removed the word *LIBRARY* from their facades under the pretext it could be intimidating and discriminatory toward a part of the population. Here, it's the same thing: reading is considered a shameful thing, a painful thing that we would like to get rid of in favour of content that requires less effort.'

Rather than discreetly part with it, the Contactual Reader then preferred to circulate the Feel-Good Book around the Reading Room. Upon contact, the Contractuals abandoned their neutrality to match their opinions with insulting comments. They read sentences, chapters, paragraphs aloud, just to make fun of them. Pointing first to a sentence, then putting a finger on the entire paragraph, each had a go with their remarks. A mocking laughter spread throughout the Reading Room, louder than I've ever heard there, a long chain of laughter of Contractual Readers making fun of non-books, and it was with renewed laughter that the Feel-Good Book was sent back to the stacks.

As for the Small Wounded Book, it had been read by the entirety of the Contractual Readers. They had even awarded it the Literature and Adversity Prize, created for the occasion. Although honoured, the Small Wounded Book declared it too much; it was, after all, just a small wounded book (laughter). It was very pleased nonetheless to have allowed the Contractuals to rediscover their taste for pleasure reading. It took the liberty of giving them some advice, it suggested some titles, some books that had influenced it, without which it would not exist, and then it went back to the stacks, exhausted but happy to have been, for a few days, wanted.

After this episode, I entrusted the Small Wounded Book to a restoration workshop that rebound it and fitted it with a leather cover. You have to see it now, it's beautiful, sturdy, solid, it looks five years younger. Within the realm of reading, it is spoken about in laudatory term, it is considered to be a good book. I am happy to see it in this state: it is making friends, it is making enemies, it is circulating, it lives again.

It was past 11 and not far from midnight. The Reading Room was cool, quiet but no longer truly silent. I had cracked the windows to let in some fresh air. Cars, scooters, buses, and elevated trains broke the silence. The Contractual Workers weren't complaining. Enough silence. The sounds of the city, at last.

Stretched out on the floor or sprawled on the sofas, the Contractuals were preparing to spend the night in the Reading Room when a synthesized voice revealed to them that the Library was about to close. In the second part of the message, the vaguely feminine voice invited them to move toward the exit as soon as possible. The tone was gentle, but the prompting firm: you have a quarter of an hour.

Five minutes later, seeing that the Contractuals were not moving, the Director came around to encourage the stragglers to be on their way.

'Leave, please, the Library is closing!'

At these words, the Contractuals donned their derby shoes or stuffed their feet into their tasselled loafers, then gathered their things, stood up yawning and, dragging their feet, made their way to the circulation desk.

It was between 11:50 and 11:55 p.m. when they asked to borrow the books they were working on, so they could finish them.

'Impossible,' I told them, repeating the standard operating procedures, 'the printed materials are fixed, they absolutely must be repatriated to the stacks before midnight, it's essential for the proper functioning of the operation.'

The Contractuals insisted, so I had to make them understand that the decision wasn't mine to make, it was non-negotiable.

'The Library is closing,' I let out through pursed lips, 'it's over, done.'

The Contractuals begrudgingly returned the books, they closed their bags, they put on their jackets, they pulled up their hoods, they said goodbye. They had to face the facts: their place was no longer here. This library, or what was left of it, was not made for them. This library was not made for me either. It was late. I was tired. I got up to close the windows. Following in the Director's footsteps, I accompanied the Contractuals to the exit.

Before closing the Library, the Director took the floor. He wanted to thank the Contractuals one last time for all the work they had accomplished. He said they could be proud. He said that many times. In the course of his speech, he insisted a lot on this notion of pride, which he coupled with that of merit. It sounded lousy. *Pride* and *merit*, vocabulary to cheaply get rid of those who have provided services for a miserable salary.

Thanks to the work of the Contractuals, all of the printed materials had been scanned, cooed the Director. The Great Library was going to write the next chapter of its history. Tomorrow, a new kind of library was to be created. A new place, one that would respond to the needs of today's readers.

Index finger raised, the Director again pronounced these three words: *innovation, information, service.* After which, the Library doors violently closed, the lights went out, the Director dissolved into the darkness.

I imagined that he remained inside the establishment to ensure sure the proper functioning of operations: turning on the night lights, switching on the surveillance cameras, and starting up the continuous humming that signalled new data entering the system. The update was programmed to begin at 12:00 a.m. and end at exactly 1:15 a.m. There wasn't a nanosecond to lose if the catalogue was to be refreshed by opening tomorrow.

Configuration.

Update.

Start.

12:00 a.m.: OK

12:27 a.m.: OK

12:53 a.m.: OK

1:14 a.m.: OK

1:15 a.m.: catalogue reactivated

The Contractual Readers, those who until now bore the name Contractual Readers, left the neighbourhood of the Great Library by the damp and dark quays. Walking along the opaque river, they thought about all these months of reading. One person wanted to talk about a book that had left an impression on her. But she was incapable of giving the title, incapable of summarizing its intention, incapable of badly quoting even one sentence, incapable of giving the name of a character, incapable of saying just two words about it. And it was the same for everyone. Despite their efforts, the former Contractuals could not manage to remember anything they had read. They had left the Library less than ten minutes ago and that was enough for them to forget the millions of pages they had read and scanned. The books, every single one of them, had gone from their heads. They continued to walk along the dark quay, realizing that it was like they had read nothing, or had read for nothing. Their reading had been stolen from them. Their memories had remained back there, in the computer system that now digested them. They walked all night while singing:

We have nothing to read
and nowhere to go
The Library is closed
it must be reinvented
We are orphans
We are orphans

Meanwhile, at the thought that a new-generation library would soon take the place of the old one, I became scared. I was scared for those who, in a second, a minute, an hour, or a year, would turn the page.

It's 9 o'clock in the morning, the doors are locked, a sign blocks the main entrance: THE GREAT LIBRARY IS TEMPORARILY CLOSED. This instruction does not only concern users: personnel are denied access, employees are sent home, and cleaning staff are invited to head to the nearest exit.

However, at ten minutes to eight, if you believe the Chief Library Clerk's testimony, everything was going well. The aforementioned was able to access his place of work as normal. He who starts at 8 a.m., who even arrives ten minutes ahead of time, proof of his unwavering commitment to public reading, has never been denied in the thirty plus years of his career.

The surveillance cameras are conclusive:

at 7:50 a.m., he presented his badge to the electronic lock located at the entrance of the parking garage;

at 7:51, he pressed the elevator button;

at 7:54, he swiped into the break room where he observed the custom that requires the first to arrive to make coffee for the entire team.

The rest of the surveillance film shows five minutes of the Stack Boss drinking his coffee in a mug emblazoned with an old photo of the Great Library accompanied by a historic slogan: TASTE THE TREASURE, 150,000 YEARS OF READING.

At 8 a.m. he is seen checking his watch, getting up to go take a peek in the hallway, and finally returning to the Break Room where he pours himself a second coffee, which he drinks this time in two swigs, then heads for the kitchen sink, rinses his cup with hot water, places it on the edge of the sink, and finally leaves the Break Room for that of the Reading, which he brings out of darkness by pressing the centralized control button.

His first task of the day is to pick up the returns carts and place the documents in baskets behind the circulation desk. But today, the first cart is empty, the second as well, same thing for the third. On the first three carts, not a single monograph, not a journal issue, no reference books. Which very clearly means that not a single document has left the shelves over the course of the past twenty-four hours.

The Stack Boss looks up.

'I don't believe it.'

In the thirty-two years of his career, he's seen some things; if he'd known his professional life was worthy of interest, he'd have written a book about it. As this idea quickly sinks in, he imagines a text teeming with anecdotes, including an entire chapter devoted to this particular day where the incredible happened: all the shelves were empty. No more dictionaries, no more encyclopedias, no more telephone books, no more journals, not a single printed document.

The Library Clerk reassures himself by saying that a redeployment exercise of the collections could have been decided on the previous evening without him being warned. The protocol is for the Head Library Clerk to be informed of any movement within the collections. But he has too much experience to ignore the fact that emergency measures, for example following leaks identified in the pipes, or any loss in watertightness, may have been taken without him being informed. Linear metres of books had been moved at the last minute without him being informed, it wasn't the first time they had done that to him.

If there is something worrying him, it's the lateness of his colleagues. At 8:19 a.m., he is, to his knowledge, the only library clerk in the establishment. Strange.

There remain forty-ish minutes until opening.

What to do while he waits?

What would a librarian do in his place?

She would check the catalogue.

In a click, he accesses the catalogue.

Search criteria: words in titles

Example: angry young book

Result: no entry.

'Not right,' says the Stack Boss, 'not right at all,' which he repeats as he does another search, drawing on different indexes, by title words, lists of titles, by subject words.

After simple searches, he moves on to combined searches, then he crosses the index by using Boolean operators AND/OR/NOT.

Balzac AND Flaubert > 0 results.
Balzac NOT Flaubert > 0 results
Balzac OR Flaubert > 0 results

Whichever title, whichever author, whichever subject he searches, no query succeeds, zero results, complete silence.

The Chief Library Clerk heads to the stacks. He begins with the Tower of Novels, then goes to inspect the other three.

He sees rows of shrubs along the shelves, a dirt path in the aisle, a stream surrounded by brambles, wild grass, and mulberries. He spots books in a bad state.

He pulls a book, opens it, flips though it. The text and images have been erased. The ink has been sucked from the book like a vampire sucks blood. The work, devitalized, is composed of blank pages.

He consults dozens of volumes like that. His heart is beating very hard.

All have met the same fate, all have become unreadable, all the pages are blank. In the span of one night, the Library has lost its printed materials, its catalogue has been wiped out, and a forest has grown in its stacks. How to inform the Director?

Returning to his office with dirty loafers, fingers scratched by brambles, the Stack Boss picks up his telephone and dials a four-digit number.

'Sir … something happened … difficult to explain … it's terrible … the books … a forest … nothing left to read.'

'Come now,' said the Director to the Stack Boss, 'you're worrying for nothing, everything is actually under control. Come to my office. I'll explain everything.'

The Director turns his computer screen in the Stack Boss's direction and invites him to follow the demonstration from the visitor's chair.

'There is no reason to panic. You haven't understood our project, that's all. You weren't brought up to date? Is that so? I'm surprised! In short, you're going to see, it's very simple. From now on, there is only one book in the catalogue, a single book, that contains all the others.'

Search criteria: title
Example: global book
Results: 1 entry

Type: Electronic document, monograph
Title(s): Global book [electronic resource]/anonymous
Type of electronic resource: text, still images
Publication: GREATLIB/LAB
Publisher: Public Establishment of the GREAT-LIB/LAB
Material description: digital file
Subject(s): all
Genre: poetry, novel, story, fiction, essay

THIS IS A PERIOD OF TRANSFORMATION THAT REQUIRES INNOVATION AND RISK. At the time of digitization, we have conceived for you a place that is innovative, pleasant, alive, secure. Welcome to the GREATLIB/LAB.

THIS IS NEW, THIS IS EXCITING, THIS IS COMPLETELY DIFFERENT. It's a new type of experience, an invitation to discover, explore, experiment. Adventure at your fingertips. Access an unknown world.

THE SPACE IS THE MESSAGE. Zones for conversation, individual niches, themed islets, reference section, modular furniture, and a wide range of colours and variety of lighting: choose your ambiance, make yourself comfortable. Founded on conviviality and intense and productive interpersonal relationships, the GREATLIB/LAB is a vast playground open 24/7. Innovative and familiar at the same time, it will very quickly feel like a second home.

COMPUTER, COMFORT, CAPPUCCINO. Whether you are an expert or novice, information professionals welcome you day and night and offer services on-demand: personalized help with research and information production, support, advice, tutorials; and for your comfort, the preparation of energy drinks and snacks à la carte.

YOU CAN'T HELP BUT SMILE WHEN YOU'RE INSIDE. Wide range of hours, availability of touch screens and cutting-edge technological equipment, collaborative practices, exceptional resources in *infotainment* and *edutainment*, likeable staff. Get caught up in the game! Get informed with a smile.

THE GLOBAL BOOK PROJECT. The heritage remains, of course, and more accessible than ever, thanks to the GLObalBOok project, recently completed. At the end of this massive project we are able to offer you 14 million books gathered into a single document! No more dispersion of content and scattering of sources. All books in one: 14 terabytes of reading. Eager to be launched into the future, the GREATLIB/LAB, in agreement with the Scientific Council and the Minister of Knowledge and Diffusion of Information, decided that from now on the collections will be closed. On that basis, no new physical book will be added to them. After focusing on changing the format of existing works and the migration of data from one medium to another, we will now focus on improving minor resources.

10:00 a.m.: launch of the GREATLIB/LAB
10:03 a.m.: entrance of guests, supervisors, financiers, scientists associated with the project
10:05 a.m.: guest reception
10:10 a.m.: social breakfast
10:15 a.m.: opening ceremony

10:16 a.m.: Director's speech: 'In Praise of Lightness'

10: 20 a.m.: philosopher's speech: 'Beyond the Library'

10:30 a.m.: presentation of GLObalBOok.

10:45 a.m.: stroll in the towers, exploration of the project 'A Green Path Through the Towers.'

12:00 p.m.: end of festivities, opening to the public.

1:15 p.m.: blackout.

1:16 p.m.: evacuation of the building.

5:00 p.m.: following heavy rainfall, a drainpipe breaks along a column, which floods part of the hall and basements.

6:00 p.m.: Management gives notice that 'technical teams are dispatched to reestablish services, but the situation is complex.'

6:15 p.m.: a second leak is found in the former Reading Room.

6:30 p.m.: the origin of the second leak is identified; corrective measures are immediately called for.

8:00 p.m.: a statement from the Management indicates that 'the opening of the GREATLIB/LAB to the public is postponed *sine die.*'

Not knowing where to go, they lingered along the quay for a while to the rhythm of their song: *We are orphans / We are orphans.* Suddenly the road opened up, the Orphans left the capital for towns, subdivisions, hamlets; arriving by surprise at a business park at the edge of a pond, they visited empty warehouses and uninhabited places; dressed in jackets and hats, they pretended to control an abandoned refinery in where, one night, they improvised a party with neither music or drinks.

Continuing their journey, they came across a ghost town, a city hall in ruins, closed places of worship, destroyed shops. Further along, in another desert, they sheltered in a house declared uninhabitable after violently inclement weather. Later they took possession of a pool that was never opened to the public due to many defects. For an entire week, they invaded a bankrupt vacation village. They were offered, instead of the countryside, burnt meadows, sad plains, polluted ponds, beaches like landfills. PRIVATE PROPERTY signs systematically barred access to woods and pine forests. The countryside was forbidden to them, the small towns proved inhospitable, and large cities were obviously too expensive. Everywhere, they just passed through.

Is there a less welcoming land? No, this land, despite being theirs, sadly, treats them like intruders. After weeks of wandering, they understood they had nowhere to live. Under these circumstances, they had no qualms about blowing up obstacles, breaking down doors, destroying gates while letting out cries of joy. When winter came, icy and wet, they hurried to build shelter for themselves out of pallets and tarps laid out on a large concrete slab. When the local militia expelled them (even the pathetic slab had an owner), they found shelter in tents, shacks, in the carcasses of cars. The good weather returned, they took up their route and made their way: *We are orphans / We are orphans.*

And then one morning, under the beautiful clear skies of the suburbs, they spotted a dark building constructed on a peninsula. Opening the metal gate by force, they found themselves in a large space. In the middle of the rubble, they discovered hundreds of books, dirty and damaged, but whole, from which they learned where they were. The Orphans had set foot in a factory that had long ago symbolized progress, which was synonymous with growth, when the words *progress* and *growth* still made sense.

During its prime, the factory was at the forefront of both industry and social struggle: one worked hard, one clashed violently, it was the seat of technological innovation and a memorable general assembly. In order to respond to the technological and commercial challenges launched by their competition, new production sites were created.

Judging this one to be out-of-date, the directors made the decision to close it. There was talk of building a contemporary art museum, then of establishing an innovation hub for the technologies of the future, then a leisure park, then an amusement park. Each project was discussed at length, but the discussions got stuck, conflicts arose, and the projects were abandoned one by one. Meanwhile, workers, foremen, and engineers had gone to join innovative places of production, the word *factory* had fallen out of use at the same time as the expression *corporate library*. They claimed that on these new sites, where space was tight, there wasn't any room for a library. The works council's budget, which was previously used as a letter of credit, lined the pockets of the *tour operators*. As for the books in the corporate library, which no one knew what to do with, they were left here, at the mercy of insects, dust, rodents.

The Orphans had unearthed a former corporate library, consisting of technical documentation and works on economic and social history. They also found a considerable number of pleasure books: short stories, gardening, cooking, sports, hobbies, travel, memoirs, and novels. Added to that were wild texts, scattered around the building: loose sheets, anonymous poems, announcements in the form of leaflets stuck on the walls. A sort of repertoire of collective thoughts, an encyclopedia of life forces, a series of measures, watchwords where books and reading were the driving force. They told of an era when the library participated in struggles, parties, and laughter.

The orphans inventoried the books, classified and shelved them on shelves built out of palettes. They opened a place that was unique, accessible, charming.

They founded the Dark Library.

The Dark Library is open Monday to Sunday, from 10 a.m. to midnight. It offers on-site browsing and allows lending. Keep your ID, chuck your proof of residence, burn your pay slips: no registration is required, no card will be delivered. The collections are free and open access.

In the absence of regulations, readers are invited to return borrowed books within a reasonable time. And if it occurs to some to not return a document, if, whether by negligence or by malice, readers keep what they have borrowed, they do not have to fear, the Dark Library will not persecute. But they must understand that this library is not meant for them.

Deprived of a budget, guardianship, and sponsorship, without public financing or private partners, it is therefore accountable to no one: with no report to submit to justify its proper use of funds, the Dark Library develops autonomously.

After the first contributions from the founding members, readers in turn left all or part of their private libraries. Therefore, collections of coherent and scholarly documents blended with small collections of pleasure reading. Here a fairy tale mixes with a war story, a nuclear physics treaty neighbours an adventure novel. Different species, generally kept apart, have been able to get closer. They talk, they argue, they fight, they debate, reflect, quarrel, they find common ground. The books here are not silent. They express themselves out loud. It's because of them if the Dark Library is noisy. To date, no one has complained.

As it still needed to develop, the Dark Library began producing its own books. Gradually, it has become a place of production for the written word. Here, on average, twenty new books see the light of day each season. At first the readers didn't think about writing; it wasn't on the agenda. It was the Dark Library that incited them to write.

Unity of place, direct access to knowledge, comfortable for the eyes, healthy atmosphere, there is no better place to make books than a library.

One morning, someone started a sentence. This sentence asserted that at least one book would always be missing from a library. Someone saw fit to comment on this first sentence. He then wrote a second, saying that a library lived as much by what it was missing and made an effort to acquire as by what it already possessed and sought to keep hold of. The second sentence called for a third, in response to the previous two: a complete library is a dead library. A fourth sentence suggested writing the missing book.

Sentence by sentence, a book took form; a book without an author's name. It's not that the members of the Dark Library refused to append their signatures, nor that in the name of intellectual freedom or vanity they wanted to remain anonymous. It's that it was impossible to know who had written what. Since everyone had a hand in the text, one sentence could very well have been written by one person and modified by another. And thus was born the Dark Library's first book.

'Who are you, little newborn book?'

'I am an orphan book.'

'Who are you, orphan book?'

'Any recognized and serious research on copyright owners will lead you nowhere. No authors, no rights, no beneficiaries. I don't know my parents' names. I was written by a thousand hands.'

'Who are you, book written by a thousand hands?'

'I am malleable, mobile, open.'

'Who are you, malleable, mobile, open book?'

'I am a poem without qualities.'

'Who are you, poem without qualities?'

'I am a poem deprived of these poetic qualities that allow people to immediately say: this is a poem. But if the reader is convinced, for some reason, that the text he has under his nose is a poem, then the poem will appear. Open your eyes wide, now listen to me.'

TO YOU OUR NAMES WOULD MEAN NOTHING

WE ARE FROM THE HAPPY FAMILY

OF ANONYMOUS READERS

WE ARE THE ORPHANS

AND WE READ WE WRITE
WE PUBLISH WE PRODUCE
WE RECEIVE WE REREAD
WE COMMENT WE REWRITE

WE ARE SWIFT AND INTREPID
WE ARE WILD AND BRAWNY
WE ARE CURIOUS AND INSATIABLE

READING LED US TO WRITING
WRITING BROUGHT US TO READING
READING DROVE US TO THE LIBRARY

BUT THE LIBRARY HAD A PROBLEM
BY THINKING ITSELF COMPLETE
IT LEFT US ORPHANS

IT WILL ALWAYS BE MISSING A BOOK
WE ARE WRITING THE MISSING BOOK

IT WILL RUN ALONG THE PATHS
IT WILL TROT ON THE TRAILS
IT WILL MOVE ALONG THE ROADS AND HIGHWAYS

IT WILL SLIDE ALONG THE ROADS, FAST AND SLOW
IT WILL TRAVEL AROUND COUNTRIES WITHOUT MAPS

AND WE READ WE WRITE

WE PUBLISH WE PRODUCE
WE RECEIVE WE REREAD
WE COMMENT WE REWRITE

A BOOK IS A PROBLEM
FOR US THERE IS ONLY ONE SOLUTION
READING AND WRITING PROBLEM BOOKS

THE FUTURE OF BOOKS IS A PROBLEM
THE PROBLEM OF BOOKS IS A QUESTION OF THE FUTURE
IT'S UP TO BOOKS TO INVENT THEIR FUTURE
THE FUTURE OF BOOKS IS IN OUR HANDS

The Monster Library is an invention of Hippolyte Martinez-Abascal.

Cyrille Martinez is a novelist and poet. He lives in Paris, where he is a librarian of French and comparative literature at the Sorbonne. He has published seven books, some of which have been adapted for theatre, and has done a number of readings in France and abroad. *The Dark Library* is his second book translated into English.

Joseph Patrick Stancil has studied French and translation at UNC-Chapel Hill and New York University. He also translated Cyrille Martinez's *The Sleepworker* for Coach House Books. He currently lives in Seattle, Washington.

Typeset in Arno and Fabrica

Printed at the old Coach House on bpNichol Lane in Toronto, Ontario, on Zephyr Antique Laid paper, which was manufactured, acid-free, in Saint-Jérôme, Quebec, from 50 percent recycled paper, and it was printed with vegetable-based ink on a 1972 Heidelberg KORD offset litho press. Its pages were folded on a Baumfolder, gathered by hand, bound on a Sulby Auto-Minabinda, and trimmed on a Polar single-knife cutter.

Translated by Joseph Patrick Stancil
Edited by Alana Wilcox
Author photo by P. Abascal
Translator photo by James Walsh
Cover design by Ingrid Paulson
Interior design by Crystal Sikma

Coach House Books
80 bpNichol Lane
Toronto ON M5S 3J4
Canada

416 979 2217
800 367 6360

mail@chbooks.com
www.chbooks.com